"I will not allow you and your entourage to invade Wyenott Towers!"

Charles de Michel's eyes flashed in his dark face.

This terrible ordeal had reduced Valentina's nerves to shreds but she had glimpsed a possible solution and out of desperation resorted to a strategem that appalled her.

"For a man who has won a most unenviable reputation before he has reached the age of thirty, you are bold indeed, cousin. When it becomes public knowledge that you have attempted to weasel out of a debt owed to a family of orphans, I'll be suprised are you not tarred and feathered and put on the next boat for—for the Khyber Pass!"

He was very still, and the look on his face made her almost sick with fear.

He said very quietly, "And you intend to see that such a tale is circulated, do you, most gentle lady? But how charming. Have you ever heard of an ugly procedure called blackmail?"

"I—h-ave also heard of a procedure called integrity. And—and human kindness." She knew her voice quivered.

After a pause that seemed endless Charles said, "I think, Madam Ruthless, you have won."

Valentina was hard put to understand why she didn't feel terribly happy.

Books by Gwyneth Moore

HARLEQUIN REGENCY ROMANCE
16–MEN WERE DECEIVERS EVER

THE DIRTY FROG
GWYNETH MOORE

Published June 1990

ISBN 0-373-31127-3

CHAPTER ONE

Herefordshire, England

Summer, 1813

"I DESPISE AND DISLIKE YOU, SIR!" Valentina Ashford made that declaration in accents of loathing. Her deeply lashed hazel eyes were frowning, and as she leaned forward, the early afternoon sunlight struck golden glints from her brown curls. "Furthermore," she added, "to bite a lady on the leg causes me to believe that you are no gentleman!"

The male she addressed fixed her with a beady eye, uttered a markedly unrepentant squawk, and scratched at the dusty ground.

Miss Ashford glanced around the deserted gardens of this pitiful estate, and observing no other human being, lifted the skirts of her primrose muslin gown and examined her abused limb. It was a nicely turned limb, well in keeping with the rest of her nicely turned self. Valentina may have reached the advanced age of one and twenty without having acquired a husband, but her vibrant beauty had attracted much attention in London. It was widely held in fact that she would have contracted a good match years ago save that she was too devoted to the care of her family to have time for suitors or the frivolities of the London Season. This observation was usually voiced with sighful regret by the gentlemen. The ladies, less inclined to hypocrisy (in this particular instance), were more likely to remark that Miss Ashford could have been a reigning toast had her dashing sire not died in the winter of 1811 of a stroke, induced by the realization that he had, in one disastrous evening, gambled away what was left of his fortune.

"I shall have a bruise, you beast," declared Valentina, accurate on both counts. "And you may be grateful you did not tear my best lace-trimmed pantalettes!"

The rooster squawked again, eyed her belligerently and strutted off.

"Roué!" said Valentina, then spun around with a gasp of fright as she heard a step behind her.

Her apprehension gave way to relief. Her new companion was no more talkative than his predecessor, but appeared to be of a far more agreeable disposition. A very small light grey donkey, with one ear perpetually at half-mast, he gave Valentina a friendly nod, and accepted her caresses.

"You are lame, I see," she said, allowing her neatly darned amber silk shawl to drift to her elbows. "I'll say one thing for you, however. You are far more polite than your owner."

The donkey looked at her forgivingly, then swished his tail and gave a snort.

"My thought exactly," said Valentina. "I did not come expecting to find a palace, you understand. But the condition of this estate could best be described as deplorable. Only look," she went on, warming to her subject, "at that perfectly dreadful barn! It sags, sir! As for the house," she turned her fine hazel eyes to the distant grandeur of the Tudor mansion, and pursed her lips. "That half-timbering is splendid—or was. Now look at it! Much of it has rotted away! The paint is a disgrace, the chimneys defy gravity, and only see how many window panes are broken! Wyenott Towers, indeed! Why not tear it down? And as for the grounds, be frank—did ever you see so many weeds? Such shameful neglect! And that hideous quarry like a red wound smack in the middle of what could have been a halfway decent park! Your master, Mr. Whatever-your-name-is, has served his home abominably. And served you little better by the look of that leg!"

"His name," said a voice of ice, "is FitzMoke. He is lame because every morning I attach a rusty chain to his leg and drag him around the quarry as a disciplinary exercise. And since neither my home, lands, nor livestock please you, madam, I shall be only too glad to escort you to your carriage."

Her heart jumping nervously, Valentina scanned the man who had come up unheard and now looked at her as from a very great height. His hair was a black untidiness about a lean dark face with a bitter mouth, hawkish nose, and strong chin. The only redeeming feature, she thought, was a pair of long and brilliant dark eyes which at the moment regarded her with pronounced distaste. Not much above average height, he was well built, his shoulders broad, his middle trim, his legs long and muscular. He wore grey riding dress and jockey boots with turned down grey cuffs. His cravat was carelessly tied, his entire appearance suggesting an impatience with fashion, yet in some odd way he looked distinguished. So this was Charles de Michel, only son of Papa's half-sister, Aunt Ruth, and her French husband, the late Henri de Michel. Although only eight and twenty he had already acquired a lurid reputation. While betrothed to a highly born lady of Quality he had run off with his neighbour's wife, then shot down and seriously wounded her husband in a duel. The betrothal, needless to say, had been at once ended. Lady Agatha had married an older, presumably wiser, viscount, which people said was a lucky escape since de Michel was now believed to be a Bonapartist.

'He looks his reputation,' thought Valentina, her heart sinking. She saw the heavy black brows pulling into a scowl, and put out her hand, saying with her brightest smile, "How do you do? Cousin."

He gripped her hand with long tanned fingers and said rudely, "So you acknowledge the relationship. You must want something." His mouth twisted. He added with a sneer. "Pray be brief, ma'am. I've little time to waste."

'What a rudesby!' thought Valentina, and promptly sat down on a rotting bench under a large and overgrown elm tree. "How fortunate that I wrote to you, Cousin Charles. You—er, do know who I am?"

"Not from the closeness of our families since we returned to these shores, certainly. But I gather you are Valentina, eldest daughter of my mother's half-brother John, who very improvidently lost all his money at the tables and left his family destitute."

Valentina's eyes flashed. Her mouth opened, then snapped shut again.

Amused, de Michel said, "Come now, do not keep your tongue between your teeth on my account. I am assured you are well acquaint with the rumours of my depravity, but there is no cause for alarm. I do not attack females. On first meeting."

"Alas," she sighed. "And we shall meet so often."

She had folded her hands in her lap. She looked small and demure and sad. And rather incredibly lovely. He had learned early that one did well to steer clear of great beauties. This one was certainly up to something. He drawled sardonically, "Have I your permission to be seated—cousin?"

"Pray do."

The gesture that accompanied those two words was queenly, and again amusement glinted in his eyes. Sitting at the far end of the bench he enquired, "Do you mean to establish a home nearby?"

"You implied," evaded Valentina, "that we did not greet you when you returned from Italy. I must protest, sir. My dear papa was most fond of your mother and spoke often of your perilous escape from The Terror. Before you removed to Rome your mama was a frequent caller at our house and—"

De Michel stared his astonishment. "Was she, so!"

"I was away at school then, and have not seen her for years." She paused, nerving herself. "As to the business that brings me here—"

"I do not discuss business matters with females, Miss Valentina," he interpolated cuttingly. "You have a brother, I believe?"

'The horrid wretch *knows* why I am here,' she thought. "Goodness me! I must acquaint you with my family." She smiled sweetly at him, and overriding his attempted protest, swept on: "My eldest brother, Lincoln, is five and twenty, and holds the rank of lieutenant. A line regiment, unfortunately, but—we have hopes, cousin."

"Do you," he said grimly. "Well—"

"My younger brother, Leslie, is nineteen. He was at Rugby, and is mad to become a Naval ensign. The poor boy is very restless, and so yearns to travel about the world."

"Indeed," growled de Michel, even more grim. "I trust you—"

"And then of course, there is my sister, Sidonie. She is seventeen now, and quite the beauty of the family, and—"

"Should have a come-out," he interjected with a sneering laugh. "And a Court gown, and—"

"But I have come to see you," she went on, her voice somewhat shrill, "because I am obliged to exercise my rights as part-owner of Wyenott Towers."

The ironic sneer was wiped away. His jaw sagged. "As—*what?*" he roared, springing to his feet. "You labour under a misapprehension, Miss Ashford! By God, but you do!''

Heavens but he had a horrid temper. Even the little donkey had gone scurrying off. Trying not to reveal how frightened she was, Valentina extracted a sheet of paper from her reticule and passed it to him.

De Michel wrenched his glare from her to the paper he held. His first shock was the recognition of his mother's hand. His second came as he read what she had written:

As security for a loan of Six Thousand Pounds, advanced to me by my brother, Mr. John Renton Ashford, I pledge a half-share in the estate known as Wyenott Towers, located north of Leominster in Herefordshire.

Signed: Ruth Gatesford de Michel
London. September 23rd, 1808.

The paper in de Michel's hand jerked, and Valentina appropriated it hurriedly. His expression murderous, he said in a voice of repressed fury, ''This is not worth a button!''

Valentina came to her feet and looked at him from under upraised brows. ''So you deny your mama's pledged word, sir.''

Seething, he clenched his fists and fought for control. ''I deny—'' he began. How disdainfully the revolting chit looked at him! He took a shuddering breath. ''I—knew nothing of this. You understand that I must consult with my mother.''

"I see. You mean to contest it." Her lip curling, she pointed out, "It is a debt of honour, Mr. de Michel."

In that moment she seemed ten feet tall, and the scorn in her eyes fairly hurled at him. He was obliged to turn away before he strangled her. "If," he said between his teeth, "your claim is substantiated, you will most certainly be repaid. Eventually."

Watching him narrowly, she murmured, "All of them?"

He spun around, his eyes wide with shock. "There are more?"

Valentina produced the others. He became perfectly white and sat down rather abruptly.

She frowned. "Are you under the hatches, Cousin Charles?"

"I am—" his voice cracked. He coughed behind his hand, apologized, and tried again. "My funds are—frozen at the present time. But—but you will be repaid, Miss Ashford."

"When?"

He ran a hand through his hair rendering it even more wild. "As soon as I can—can liquidate—er, some properties. If necessary."

"I fear that will not do."

He sprang up again as though suddenly realizing she was still standing. "It shall have to do, madam! I am temporarily embarrassed." He flushed painfully. "In order to raise such a sum—"

"With interest," she pointed out sweetly. "Going back several years in some instances."

"My God," he snarled. "You're a regular cents-percenter, you money-grubbing little—"

"Temper, temper," admonished Valentina, but the rage in the dark eyes caused her to step back a pace.

De Michel said in a harsh strained voice, "Why a'God's name did not your father come to me years ago with these notes? One of them goes back to 1805! Before we went to Italy! If I'd but known!"

"Good gracious, sir, does it not occur to you to be grateful? Your mama evidently judged the need desperate, and my papa, the most generous, warmhearted of men, obliged her."

"Meaning to gouge her later for interest? His own flesh and blood!"

"My father, sir, had absolutely no intention of gouging the lady. I doubt if he ever meant to—" She broke off hurriedly.

"To call in the notes? But you do, eh?"

Her eyes fell. Papa would not have wanted this. She said in a suddenly wavering voice, "My need, cousin, is as great as was your mama's when she came to us."

He gave a derisive snort. "I doubt that. Oh, never fly into the boughs again. You'll get your money. Only, it will take time."

"Time, sir, is what I have none of."

Despite her brave words, tears had beaded on her lashes. De Michel said in a gentler voice, "Assuming that to be true, what would you suggest I do? It will likely take me a week or so to raise six thousand pounds."

She thought, 'Good heavens! He really *is* under the hatches!' "I do not want your money, Mr. de Michel," she said.

He gave a gasp. "But— Then what the deuce *do* you want?"

"You own a very nice house on—" she gulped "—on Hill Street."

His face became bleak. "It is worth considerably more than these vowels, madam. Furthermore, it is closed."

"Then open it. I am not asking for the Deed, only that you allow us to live there rent-free for a time. We will not be a charge on you."

Again there appeared the mocking grin that twisted his mouth and left his eyes coldly unamused. "Oh, will you not? Have you any notion of the size of that house, ma'am? Do you know how many servants are required to maintain it? How much it costs in candles and in coal? Besides, from the look of you, your entire wardrobe would have to be replenished before you could dare walk out on the flagway! Oh, how the old tabbies would stare!"

Scarlet with embarrassment, Valentina leapt to her feet. "Do you know, cousin, how easy it would be for me to thoroughly dislike you?"

"Yes." He gave a careless shrug. "I've no doubt you have taken me in deep aversion. My apologies if I am too blunt for you. But you cannot have the house in Town. No, never argue. For many reasons I cannot open it. You shall have to wait for me to raise the funds."

"I tell you I *cannot* wait!" Sudden tears scalded her eyes. In a cracked and shaking voice, she said, "Don't you understand—you horrid, *horrid* man? We have nowhere to go! I *cannot* impose on poor Tibby any longer! I must find a—a place to take my sister and brother, and...I just can't!"

De Michel drew back uneasily. "For heaven's sake, don't do that! I'm sure we can contrive something." He stopped. Those great hazel eyes had fixed on a spot over his shoulder.

A small impatient hand wiped the tears away. "Hmm..." she said.

De Michel glanced behind him. "No! By the Lord Harry—no!"

Valentina extended an imperious hand. He gave up his snowy handkerchief reluctantly, and she blew her nose, then tucked the handkerchief in her reticule. "Do you live there?"

"Certainly not! It hasn't been occupied for ten years. Do you think I'd allow my mother to dwell in such a ruin? We live in what was the steward's cottage, half a mile to the west, and— Where are you going?"

"To have a look," said Valentina.

"WELL?" SNEERED DE MICHEL, looking up at Valentina from the dusty and dilapidated entrance hall.

"Ill!" she countered, coming gingerly down the stairs and looking sadly at the missing posts in the railing, the thick cobwebs, the smoke stains over the chimney, the water stains on the ceiling. "How *could* you have allowed such a fine old house to go to rack and ruin like this?''

He said with the twisted smile she already loathed, ''Yes, is it not—'deplorable'? The half-timbering sagging, the paint peeling, the window panes broken! 'Wyenott tear it down?' Your own words, ma'am. The furnishings have been under holland covers for so long they're likely thoroughly rotted. No one can live in this poor hovel until I have it restored and brought up to style, and even then there will still be that 'hideous quarry—smack in the middle of what could have been a halfway decent park.' *N'est-ce pas?*''

Ignoring his sarcasm, she murmured thoughtfully, ''It could be made a lovely home. When do you mean to start the work of restoration?''

His lips tightened. ''When I am in funds again, madam.''

''Which may be a very long time, I collect. I've a better idea, Cousin Charles. Let us live here, and we will start the restoration for you.''

He threw back his head and laughed heartily. ''Two girls and a nineteen-year-old chub of a boy? I wish I may see it!''

''Your wish is my command, sir. My sister and I can scrub and clean, for a start. We've one faithful retainer left who is very clever with his hands. And my brother is not a chub, but a—''

''A first-rate carpenter? An experienced house painter? A plumber? I've yet to find a young gentleman of Quality capable of doing anything remotely as worthwhile!''

"And at which of those worthwhile skills do you excel, cousin?"

His chin lifted. He drawled, "I've more important things to do with my time than to perform menial tasks, madam. And this conversation is ridiculous! By no stretch of the imagination, will I allow you and your entourage to invade Wyenott Towers!"

This terrible ordeal had reduced poor Valentina's nerves to shreds, but she had glimpsed a possible solution and out of desperation resorted to a stratagem that appalled her. "For a man who has won a most unenviable reputation before he has reached the age of thirty, you are bold indeed, cousin. When it becomes public knowledge that you have attempted to weasel out of a debt owed to a family of orphans I'll be surprised are you not tarred and feathered and put on the next boat for—for the Khyber Pass!"

He was very still, and the look on his pale, set face made her almost sick with fear.

He said very quietly, "And you intend to see that such a tale is circulated, do you, most gentle lady? But how charming. Have you ever heard of an ugly procedure called blackmail?"

"I h-have also heard of a procedure called integrity. And—and human kindness." She knew her voice had quavered. He was staring at her with such contempt she felt the tears well up again and fought them back bravely.

"I think, Madam Ruthless, you have won," he said after a pause that seemed endless. "But—do not think to move in and then rest on your laurels! *I* will set your tasks and *I* will make regular inspections. If the work is not performed to my satisfaction and within one month's time—you will have forfeited your bargain, and blackmail or not, out you go and you shall have to wait for your money! Do you accept my terms, Miss Ashford?''

Very pale, Valentina croaked, ''I accept, Mr. de Michel.''

IN RESPONSE TO DE MICHEL'S RING the butler made his stately way into the parlour. A tall man of considerable girth, his double chins gleamed with perspiration on this hot afternoon. Madame, he advised sonorously, was ''on the terrace. That being the only cool place in this—establishment.''

De Michel fixed him with a cold stare. ''Do not curl your lip at this house, Watkyns. It is adequate for us all on a temporary basis. You'd have something to grumble at had I installed us in the Towers.''

Flushed, and vibrating with outrage, Watkyns bowed and took himself off to advise Monsieur Jean-Louis that the master was in one of his rages again.

De Michel, meanwhile, made his way to the small rear terrace of this large and quite charming house. Madame Ruth, his mother, lay on a chaise longue, and for a moment he stood frowning down at her. Her eyes were closed, and she was fanning herself lazily, the dappled light slanting through the beech trees to flicker across her graceful figure. At nine and forty Ruth de Michel was still a remarkably beautiful woman. The fair ringlets charmingly arranged at each ear were touched with silver, but her clear skin was unwrinkled, the high cheekbones, thin straight nose and finely cut lips as sure to win admiring glances today as when they had brought her the title of Goddess of London some thirty years earlier. Tall and willowy, she had kept her figure, and the very low-cut silken gown of a pale blue-green drew attention to her ample and snowy bosom.

She opened her magnificent blue eyes drowsily, smiled up at him and put out one white hand. "You have come to share some of your time with me. How very kind. You must stay." She patted the chaise beside her. "*Je vous en supplie!* I am ennui, Charles. But positively ennui. This desolation to which you condemn me is so—desolate! I shall go mad." She frowned and added thoughtfully, "Tomorrow, perhaps. So be warned, my handsome son."

He chuckled, sat beside her, and lifted her hand to his lips. "Do not be wasting your charm on your far from handsome son, *chère Maman*."

"You are most certainly handsome," she argued indignantly. "Especially when you smile. No son of your dear papa could dare be otherwise. Besides—" her soft fingertips caressed his cheek "—it is not a waste if I employ my undisputed charm to win you from your black mood. What has you in a dudgeon today, love? Are the builders' estimates too high? Do the villagers grumble again? Is the Reverend Mr. Tembury complaining about the church roof? Is the Home Farm sinking malodorously into the duck pond? What? Pray tell, for I am fascinated by such earth-shaking events.''

"All of those," he said, with the slow smile that so transformed his features. He patted the slender hand he held, and stared down at it, then glanced at her from under his heavy brows. "Can you truly be ennui, my dear? You were at the Whitcomb garden party on Friday, the Luttrell's river breakfast on Saturday, we entertained Lord and Lady Norton and the Rogers clan for dinner and cards last evening, and—"

"And they are all such *crushing* bores," she sighed. "Oh, Charles—if you but *knew* how I miss civilization! The wits and the wags, the sophisticated chatter—"

"Gossip," he qualified ironically.

"All the gaiety and excitement and entertainments of my beloved London! If you could only understand how unhappy I am."

A muscle flickered in his jaw. He said, "Do not underrate me, Mama."

She met his eyes levelly. After a moment of tense silence, he added, "And I am perfectly willing to take you shopping whenever you wish it."

"But—"

"But that is all, Mama."

The thinner line of his lips, the grimness in his face, warned her. Sighing, she withdrew her hand. "I did not dream when you were a charming small boy that you would grow up to be my cruel gaoler."

He stood and walked a few paces from her to gaze across the tranquil gardens. "Not that, surely? I try to ensure that you want for nothing."

"Save that which I want the most! My old friends. My family."

"You mean Papa's family."

"Is it a crime that I adored my dear husband?" Her voice was sharper now and there was a flash in her eyes. "As a child you were jealous of our love. Must you now resent the fact that I also love his people?"

One of his hands clenched. After a minute he said quietly, "You forget perhaps, that I loved him, too." He turned to face her again and went on in a lighter manner, "And since you miss your family so much, you will be pleased to hear that I was talking to someone today who—er, knew my Uncle John."

Madame made a pretty moue and yawned behind her hand.

"So much for filial affection," he said drily. "I had thought you most fond of the gentleman."

"Oh, I was, I suppose. Only he was such a baby."

"Did he not in fact fund you on several occasions?"

Madame sat up straight and began to tidy her ringlets. "On numerous occasions." She glanced at him. "Does that displease you, Charles?"

"Should it, my dear?"

"I don't know. You are so harsh at times." She straightened the zephyr shawl about her elbows. "Poor John. One does tend to forget past kindnesses. His was a truly generous heart. And he died penniless."

His eyes very keen but his voice mild, de Michel murmured, "Egad, ma'am. For how long did this financial exchange continue?"

"We borrowed from each other on a regular basis for years."

"Before we went to Italy?"

"And after we returned. Your father never knew, but when John was in the basket he came to me, and when I was out of funds, I went to him. Dear John. He never denied me."

She stood and shook out her skirts. "I must go and change. I dine with the vicar this evening, you know. La, but what a giddy social flight!" Starting away, she turned back when he called after her.

"*Maman,* be frank. Am I deep in debt to the Ashfords?"

"If there is an indebtedness," she said, her serenity restored, "it is rather on the other side of the coin. Not that I kept very close watch on our transactions, but I fancy my emerald pendant more than tipped the scales in our favour."

De Michel gave a gasp. "You gave—Uncle John the—the Gatesford emerald? My God! Do you know the value of— Ah—but you hoax me. You wore it on Saturday evening."

"I wore the copy. Oh yes, I had a copy made. Grandpapa Gatesford was alive then, and would have been distressed otherwise, and I could not refuse John when he was so anxious to invest in that funny little German man's scheme for light or heat, or whatever it was. Though I expect most of the proceeds went over the gaming tables. Still, I believe the emerald was worth far more than the loans I had made from John."

"I believe...you are correct...." said de Michel feebly.

Curious, she asked, "What is it? Are you very angry about it?"

"No, no. In point of fact it releases me from quite an unpleasant...obligation. Although..." He paused, smiled in what she thought an odd way, then burst into hilarious laughter.

"Good gracious," gasped the lovely Madame Ruth. "Whatever is it?"

"Oh *Maman,*" he gasped, wiping tears from his eyes. "I believe I am going to teach somebody a very well-deserved lesson! By Jupiter, but I am!"

CHAPTER TWO

"My...dear...God!" Mr. Leslie Ashford halted in
the entrance hall of Wyenott Towers and looked about
him. He was a tall, loose-limbed youth with regular
features, thickly curling brown hair, and a bright,
energetic disposition. Just now, his fine green eyes re-
flected stark horror, and his comely face was pale. "I
thought the *outside* was bad enough," he gasped.

Shrinking in behind him, Sidonie, petite and lovely,
gave a wail. "Oh! How *horrid!* Tina—we cannot live
in *this!* You cannot ask it of us!"

"Cheer up, both of you," said Valentina, carrying
two buckets and mops from the loaded waggon. Horace had swept the floors and removed the holland
covers, at least in the entrance hall, creating a vast
improvement over her first sight of this house. She
wondered what they'd have said had they seen it then.
She said bracingly, "Our furniture reached here safely,
and Horace has been working hard." Ashford slanted
a shocked look at her, and she said hurriedly, "I know
it is not elegant, but—"

"Elegant!" Sidonie's big green eyes filled with
tears. "It is ghastly!"

"A long way from May Fair." Ashford slid an arm
about his little sister. He was deeply attached to all his

family, but there was a special closeness between him and Sidonie, even as there was between Valentina and Lincoln.

"A thousand miles from *anywhere!*" sobbed Sidonie, leaning her face against his sleeve. "Oh—Leslie, I shall die! I shall shrivel up and *die!*"

"Well, don't die in here, child." Lady Clara Rustwick bustled in with her Pekingese under one plump arm and a carpet-bag in her free hand. "We shall have to scrub at least one bedchamber before we can lay you out."

Ashford managed a grin, and Valentina gave her large aunt a grateful smile.

"H-How can you…joke?" wept Sidonie. "We are caught up in a—nightmare, do you not see?"

"I see that your sister is looking properly gutfoundered," said her ladyship, who was known for her salty vocabulary. "As well she might, poor sweet." She raised her voice and howled, *"Horace!"*

An odd mixture of thumps and footsteps announced the arrival of a brawny man who staggered in, heavy laden, his peg-leg bouncing little puffs of dust from the floorboards. "Here…m'lady," he panted. "All present and…correct, marm."

"Present, anyway," qualified Ashford, looking gloomily at the clouded windows.

"First things first," decreed Lady Clara, depositing the Pekingese on the floor and the carpet-bag on a rickety sideboard. "We must have tea. Where is the kitchen, Tina? Horace, is the stove lit?"

"Yes marm, and the kettle on the hob."

Barking shrilly, the Pekingese made a sudden dart for the stairs.

"A rat!" shrilled Sidonie.

"No—was it?" Ashford brightened. "Mandy will get him, I'll wager!"

"Mandarin!" shouted my lady. "I want no rats eaten!"

In full cry, Mandarin and Ashford departed on the hunt.

More feet sounded in the dilapidated hall.

"Look!" wailed Sidonie. "That is the last—the absolutely *last* straw!"

"No it ain't," said her brother from the landing. "It's a donkey, Sid. What a nice little chap."

Mandarin reappeared, flopping down the staircase in hot pursuit of a fat mouse.

Lady Clara gave a shriek as the rodent whizzed across her foot.

Sidonie lapsed into screaming hysterics.

FitzMoke brayed and departed the scene hurriedly.

"Well, well," drawled de Michel, moving back from the front doors as mouse, dog, and donkey shot past. "I see you're getting settled. How nice."

He strolled inside, ignoring Sidonie who had sunk to her knees and was screaming lustily.

Ashford advised his little sister that she was making a cake of herself, then helped her up and put his arms around her.

"That's better," said de Michel as the uproar subsided.

Gritting her teeth, Valentina performed the introductions.

De Michel bowed. "Do you mean to stay here also, Lady Clara? We have small acquaintance, but I fear this must not be the—er, atmosphere to which you are accustomed."

"When one has meagre funds, one adjusts," said my lady, her shrewd eyes taking in every inch of this notorious nephew. "I would call this a ruin rather than an atmosphere. Even so, we are grateful for your generosity in allowing us to stay here."

De Michel had the grace to flush and with the gesture of a fencer acknowledging a hit, bowed.

"It is certainly no worse than living cramped up as we was with Mrs. Tibbetts," her ladyship continued. "Perhaps you recall my brother-in-law's housekeeper? She and her husband own a neatish farm in Sussex, and was so good as to take us in, but nine people in a house built for four is enough to drive anyone to blue ruin. This is some improvement. However dilapidated."

"And however temporary," murmured de Michel blandly.

"My sister told us of your—bargain, sir," said Ashford, whose pride was galled by the arrangement. Reluctantly, he held out one hand while he kept the other arm about Sidonie.

De Michel's grip was brief and hard, and a wicked amusement glinted in his dark eyes. "Don't like it, do you?"

Ashford flushed. "No, sir. I don't. But—beggars can't be choosers. We shall do our best to meet your terms."

"Indeed, I hope you can. But as I told your sister, my standards are high and time is short."

Sidonie turned a shocked and tear-stained face to peep at de Michel. Her eyes widened, then she buried her head against her brother's chest again.

Ashford said with stiff resentment, "We've not yet moved in. Cousin."

"And are eager to get started I fancy." De Michel slanted a pointed glance at the wilting Sidonie. "I must not delay you."

Horace reappeared with word that the tea was made, and looked at the visitor uncertainly. Valentina introduced their faithful retainer, sure that de Michel would snub him. He surprised her by taking the sturdy man's hand, giving him an astonishingly warm smile and saying, "Army, were you? Is that how you lost your leg?"

"Yussir. In '99."

De Michel echoed thoughtfully, "'99 ... Were you in the Egmont-op-Zee action then?"

"That I were, sir," nodded Horace, beaming.

"Were you, by Jove! Then you served with Sir John Moore! What a splendid fellow he must have been."

"Splendid's the only word for him, sir, and that's no lie! Sir John was the finest officer I ever knew. He *built* the 52nd, Mr. de Michel, and it'll do him honour in this war, you mark my words!"

De Michel said he had no doubt of it, and bowing to the ladies, took his leave.

"Top lofty bounder, ain't he," grunted Ashford. "I wonder he didn't bring his whip."

"He didn't want any part of this," Valentina said honestly. "I forced it on him. He likely despises me."

Ashford flared, "With his reputation he has no right to despise anyone!"

"At least you found a roof to put over our heads, love." Lady Clara added with a faint smile, "I wonder if his mama knows about all this."

Tired, silent, and discouraged, they followed Horace across the hall, around to the right, along a dark passage, and into a vast and dreary kitchen.

"Good gracious me," muttered Lady Clara.

"What a barn," said Ashford.

"Tea...!" sighed Valentina rapturously. "Oh thank you, Horace."

Sidonie sniffed and wiped her eyes. "You never told us he is so very handsome," she murmured.

BY THE END OF THAT WEEK they had cleaned out cupboards and drawers, swept and scrubbed the kitchen, dining and withdrawing rooms, appropriated their various bedchambers on the first floor, integrated their charming articles of furniture with those pieces remaining in the house, and dispossessed some starlings which had taken up residence in a tower bedroom.

Ashford worked with Horace in boarding up broken windows until new glass could be installed, replacing fallen half-timbering, repairing sagging cupboard doors, missing stair railings, and shelving. Sidonie wept for her lost London, proclaimed herself little better than an unpaid servant, helped with the cooking, and managed to do as little as possible. Valentina, Lady Clara, and Horace worked long and hard, with the result that coming slowly downstairs that Friday afternoon, Valentina felt a little glow of pride.

The staircase descended in a grand sweep to the centre of the entrance hall. The handrail needed refinishing, but at least it was no longer thick with dust and cobwebs. Sunlight slanted across the gleaming parquet floors below; the credenza beside the front doors held a large bowl of flowers which Sidonie had gathered from the weedy gardens. The odour of dust and damp had given way to the tang of beeswax, the smell of dinner from the kitchen, the scent of the flowers. This poor old house was beginning to feel like a home.

"Well, I shall not! I have worked until my poor nails are broken and my hands are all red! I am going for a walk!" Sidonie's distant voice rang with indignation and the side door slammed.

Valentina sighed. Horace had been deserted again. But to be snatched from Town when she had reached the age at which she should have had her come-out, was hard for little Sidonie. Particularly since so many of her friends had made their bow to Society this year, and more would do so next Season.

Footsteps sounded on the outside steps. De Michel had warned her he would come to check on their progress. Well, he would see! With a little thrill of anticipation, she snatched the mob-cap from her head, ran down the remaining stairs, and peered anxiously at her reflection in the fine old mirror that hung over the Chinese chest they had brought from Town. She moaned. Her hair was crushed and untidy, and there was a streak of grime down one cheek. She tidied frantically and flew to answer the knock at the door.

Her lower lip sagged a little. A tall lady waited, her elegance shielded by the dainty parasol she held. Her walking dress was of creamy beige batiste, the long sleeves threaded with the same scalloped brown satin ribbon which trimmed the front openings. The overdress was buttoned to the waist, then hung loosely to reveal the cream silk robe beneath, the frilled hem trimmed with matching brown ribbon. Her bonnet, of brown straw, was tied with cream ribbons. The poke, edged with cream lace, framed fair ringlets dusted with grey, an exquisite face and big blue eyes that held a wistful smile.

In a soft, beautifully modulated voice, the caller asked if Miss Ashford was at home, and presented a small calling card.

"I—am Miss Ashford," stammered Valentina, and glanced at the card. *Madame Henri de Michel*. "My goodness! You are my Aunt Ruth!" Confused, and horrifyingly aware that she had neglected to remove her apron, she blushed scarlet, and glancing up met such a kind look that she gave a helpless shrug and said, "You must think me a proper widgeon, ma'am. Pray come in!"

Madame gave an enchanting little chuckle, folded her parasol and passed it to the liveried footman who waited on the lower step. Valentina ushered them inside, snatched off the apron, and gave a tug on the bellrope.

Uncooperatively the bellrope fell from its wire and flopped over her head. Madame uttered a little cry. The footman uttered a strangled snort. Disentangling herself, Valentina could have sunk.

"I fear," she gulped, knowing her face must glow like a beacon, "that I am unable to summon my servant. Your man will l-like to go to the kitchen and have a cup of tea, I feel sure." She gave him hurried directions, and managed to escape his twitching face by turning to beg that her aunt be seated. "Will you take tea, ma'am? Or a glass of lemonade, perhaps?"

"I will first take a hug from my dear niece." Madame's eyes scarcely shifted downward, but with a faint moan Valentina remembered, and relinquished her clutch on the rotted bellrope before she was wrapped in a scented embrace, and a kiss pressed upon her cheek. Holding her at arm's length, Madame Ruth observed, "You are lovelier by far than Charles described you. Indeed, you put me very much in remind of your dear mama. And you have John's eyes, lucky child." Gracefully occupying the least offensive chair, she went on, "Do you remember me at all, Valentina?"

"I didn't remember that you were so very beautiful," said Valentina shyly.

Madame laughed her musical laugh. "You have enslaved me at one blow! My goodness, how grown-up you are! You were always away at school, or visiting friends or some such thing when I came calling—so many years ago. Faith, but I could not believe it when Charles told me you were here. How dreadful of him to have condemned you to dwell in this monstrous ruin. Whatever must you think of us?"

So he hadn't told her the whole truth. Relieved, Valentina explained, "We were in rather desperate straits, ma'am. Cousin Charles was most reluctant to let us move in here, but did so at my—ah, urging. Indeed, we are most grateful."

Madame leaned forward and patted Valentina's hand. "You are too gracious. My son can see no fault in this old place and has more plans for it than are likely to be accomplished, alas. Good heavens, child! Whatever have you been about? Your poor nails!"

Valentina snatched her hand away hurriedly. "We have been— That is—the removal from Sussex, you know, was—"

"Sussex? But—do you no longer live on Chester Street? Never say you lost the Town house?"

"Well—er—"

"Oh, my poor dear! But you referred to your 'man'. So you do still have servants?"

Valentina gave up. "We are, as my brother would say, quite in the basket, Aunt Ruth. Horace was given work by my papa years ago. No one else would employ him because he had lost a leg while serving as a light dragoon. He has stayed with us ever since, whether or not he is paid, and is the soul of loyalty."

Blinking incredulously, Madame gasped, "But the Towers was *filthy!* Do you say that *you* have done all this menial labour?"

"No, no. Not alone, ma'am. My family and I."

"If *ever* I heard of such a thing!" Madame's glorious eyes flashed. "Charles might at least have sent our servants to make the house ready for you! He will hear from me, I promise you! It is quite typical! Because he loves this grisly wilderness he thinks it divine for the rest of us! I am in little better case than you, sweet child, for he keeps me buried here, denied my friends, my dear London and all her excitements and—" She started, and as if realizing she had said more than she meant, added, "But never heed me. I am silly at times, and Charles means only the best. You must not be thinking him a despot."

Considerably startled, Valentina made a polite response, and the conversation progressed along more orderly lines. It soon became clear however, that this beautiful woman was desperately lonely and unhappy. Her own burdens seeming less crushing, Valentina longed to cheer her, and when the time came to part, expressed the hope that her gracious visitor would soon come again. "I wish you might join us for a little dinner party, Aunt Ruth. But at the present time I fear we do not entertain."

Madame patted her cheek fondly. "The thought is what counts, my dear. And as for dinner parties, I should give one for you, but—alas, I am not permitted such frivolities."

Once again her eyes were full of sorrow. Astounded, Valentina did not know what to say, and was relieved when another voice exclaimed,

"Ruth de Michel! Can I believe my eyes?" Lady Clara surged down the stairs and came towards them, her broad cheeks flushed, her smile as bright as the glitter in her eyes.

"Clara," trilled Madame, stooping to kiss the air beside her sister-in-law's ear. "How many years it has been! To think you are still able to care for your dear sister's children. You look—why I vow you are *thinner,* love!"

Lady Clara, who had put on thirty-five pounds since last they met, ignored this home thrust, and purred with a beaming smile, "I cannot credit you would venture so far from London's noise and nonsense. A repairing lease, my dear? You do look a little pulled. Have you been ill?"

'Oh dear, oh dear,' thought Valentina.

THE AFTERNOON WAS WARM, the sun beamed from a deep blue sky to brighten emerald meadows thickly dotted with Ryeland sheep, to sparkle on the smooth serenity of the River Wye, to strike fire from red rock and throw into sharp relief richly forested hills, and westward, the higher mountains of Wales. Truly, a sight to delight the eyes and warm the heart of any English man or woman, but the slender girl in the light green muslin gown wandered with head down, and eyes that saw only Hyde Park and St. James's; the mansions of May Fair; the latest in fashions, and that holy of holies to which only in her yearning dreams would she ever be admitted—Almack's. Tears dimmed her green eyes as she pondered the unkindness of fate. Lucilla and Monica and Anne would make their come-outs next Season and were already planning their Court gowns and their parties. And Lucilla was plain, Monica had a squint, and Anne was pretty enough but inclined to throw out spots when she became nervous. Why should they be so fortunate as to have rich parents, while she, prettier than all of them put together, was doomed to isolation and poverty in this horrid rural desert? Nobody gave a button if she cried herself to sleep every night. Valentina had made herself into an old maid drudge, and Aunt Clara was so fat and insensate that nothing ever penetrated her bovine complacency.

Sidonie bit her lip with a twinge of conscience. They were both fond of her—in their way. But neither had the faintest understanding of her misery, and even Leslie, as dear as a brother could be, didn't really appreciate her loneliness. What was life without one's friends? Without the handsome boys who had flocked around and adored her in Town? What was there here? Nothing but quiet and boredom. No one to chatter with but her own family, for who would call or have anything to do with the poor relations Charles de Michel had installed in his wretched old ruin? And even if they did, who would they be? Nobodies.

Country bumpkins who wouldn't know a minuet from a marzipan!

She glanced up and halted. Goodness, but she must have walked a long way! This part of the estate looked quite well-kept and prosperous. There was a farm some distance ahead. Perhaps the Home Farm where Leslie went to purchase their dairy goods, and which he had said enthusiastically was "a jolly fine place." She detected a movement. A horseman, coming this way. And she was all alone! It was most improper for her to be without a chaperon, especially so far from what now served as "home." She retreated deeper into the shade of the trees. The horse was spirited, and the gentleman a splendid rider, whoever he was. The big black shied suddenly. The rider kept his seat, but his hat went flying. He swung from the saddle to retrieve it, and she recognized the dark hair, the athletic build. De Michel! He was fully occupied as the horse sidled and danced and tried to keep him from remounting. Sidonie ran quickly from the dappled shade, and sat down on the grass. She spread her skirts so that just a glimpse of her pantalettes could be seen, then lay back in a graceful pose, and closed her eyes.

A moment later she heard the approaching hoof-beats. Her heart thudded as they quickened to a gallop. Good heavens—was he blind? Surely he wouldn't ride right over her? She recollected then that she wore the green muslin and the grass was quite long. She was likely all but invisible, and he was coming straight for her—at speed! With a squeak of fear, she sat up.

A ringing neigh, a shout, a thud, and the diminishing pound of hooves.

"Damn and blast!" roared de Michel, sprawled among the meadow grasses.

"Oh!" gasped Sidonie, one hand flying artistically to her bosom. "*How* you frightened me!"

Clambering to his feet and brushing mud from his garments he swore under his breath. He had wrenched his ankle and it throbbed fiercely. He swore again as a cut on the heel of his hand left a vivid bloodstain on his moleskin breeches. Furious, he glared at the alarmed beauty and demanded, "What in the *devil* are you doing out here? Enjoying a jolly summer's picnic?" He glanced around, thirsting for battle, but could see no sign of her family.

His hair was tumbled, there was a scrape on his left cheekbone, and his dark eyes were stormy with anger. Sidonie thought him quite the most handsome and fascinating man she ever had met, and said in a trembling little voice, "I w-went for a walk, and became lost. I was so tired I lay down to rest—"

"Clever," he interpolated cuttingly. "As well as being hoydenish in the extreme. You are fortunate I was the one you unhorsed, Miss Impropriety."

She took refuge in tears, a sure captivator of helpless males. "I am s-so sorry, Cousin Charles."

"Don't snivel," he growled. "You were snivelling when first I saw you!"

Perhaps this man was less fascinating than she'd thought. She blinked her great, tear-gemmed eyes at him. He had come closer and was scowling down at her. He really did look romantic. She lifted a trembling little hand and tried again. "Won't you p-please help me up, sir?"

De Michel was tempted to ask if she'd broken a leg, but restrained himself and took her hand. He pulled, she strove, and predictably lurched against him.

"Oh, my," she exclaimed, clutching his cravat and blushing rosily.

He looked down at her. Gad, but she was a lovely little thing....

"I GATHERED you were not friends, exactly," teased Valentina, taking the pegs from the sheet and struggling to control it as the breeze sent it billowing.

Working at the far end of the clothes-line in the service yard beyond the row of poplars, Lady Clara took down a towel, sniffed it, then put it up again. "These will need more time, love," she called cheerily. "My, don't they smell nice? I've always wondered what it was like to hang up and bring in one's own wash. There's quite a knack to it, though. Such a pity that we didn't put the prop up in just the right way this morning."

"Yes, but at least all these weeds kept some of the things from falling in the dirt. Now do not fob me off, dear. Why do you not cry friends with my Aunt Ruth?"

Lady Clara eyed a knitted pair of unmentionables uneasily. "These look smaller," she muttered. "I wonder if we should have boiled them.... Oh well, they're dry at all events. I do not cry friends with Ruth de Michel," she went on, "because I loathe and abominate the woman."

Valentina ceased doing battle with a large tablecloth and stared at her aunt's broad flushed features in no little surprise. "Why—I never heard you say that of anyone. She is so lovely—"

"Aye, and knows it! The gentlemen are putty in her hands. Henri de Michel was as good as betrothed to your Aunt Cecily—until Ruth saw him."

"Is that why poor Aunt Cecily never married? Yet everyone says that Uncle Henri and Aunt Ruth were devoted."

"Oh, she loved him. I won't deny that. But she'd not—" She paused, wrinkling her nose. "My muffins!" she wailed and went off at an ungainly trot, her ample skirts flapping as she made for the kitchen.

Left alone, Valentina took down the clothes that were sufficiently dry and bundled them into the clothes basket, then did battle with the prop again. Who would have dreamed it so difficult to balance a long pole so as to hold the clothes-lines from sagging? The beastly thing always slid the wrong way. She was flushed and heated when at last she picked up the basket. It was quite heavy and she sighed a little. She was rather tired and there seemed no end to the tasks yet to be accomplished. Guilt seized her. Her prayers had been answered; they had found a safe harbour, at least for a time, and all she could do was grumble. She glanced at the building clouds and sent a small apology heavenward. Making her way absently around to the front of the house, she wondered if there was more to what Aunt Clara had said of Madame Ruth. Not that Aunt Clara would tell a fib exactly, but she would be quick to resent any slight to her younger sister Cecily. Her own marriage had been a happy one, although childless, but she had always grieved that Cecily had gone a spinster to her early grave. The most generous and caring lady imaginable was Aunt Clara, but—

"Allow me to be of assistance, pretty one."

A blue-clad arm appropriated the basket. A tall, powerfully built gentleman kept pace with her, admiration in his grey eyes. Probably in his late thirties, he wore a high-crowned beaver hat with thick sandy hair curling below it. His complexion was florid, his countenance rather harsh but not unpleasing. He was dressed more for town than country in blue superfine, dove grey pantaloons and black Hessians. Spurs jingled at his heels and a fine chestnut horse was tethered at the foot of the steps.

Before the startled Valentina could do more than take in these details, he asked, "Is your employer at home, lass?"

"Did you wish to see Lady Rustwick, sir?"

He looked surprised. "Gad, is she here, too?"

Irritated by his manner, Valentina said coolly, "Lady Rustwick, Mr. Leslie Ashford and Miss Sidonie Ashford reside here, sir. I am Miss Ashford."

He halted abruptly and stood staring at her, obviously taken aback. "By...Jove!" His gaze travelled her windblown hair, her heated face, the grimy apron and simple muslin round gown. "Well if that

don't beat the Dutch! I thought you was the wash-
er—'' He cut the words off hurriedly.

Valentina's chin lifted. ''I presume you have something more cogent than that to remark, sir.''

Smothering a grin, he rested the laundry basket on
the terrace, took out his cardcase and handed her a
card reading, Derwent Aloysius Locks, Bart. ''My
apologies,'' he said, removing his hat and bowing.
''But I cannot but be astonished to see a lady per-
forming the tasks of a menial.''

Flushing, Valentina said, ''We have met with financial reverses, Sir Derwent. I am only grateful that
Mr. de Michel allows us to live here.''

His grey eyes shot to the house. He whispered
''Jove!'', then grinned engagingly. ''I am your neighbour, ma'am. When I heard a family had moved into
this—er, the Towers, I thought perhaps de Michel had
restored the old place. If there is anything I can do to
be of service...''

''You are very kind. Perhaps you would care for a
glass of lemonade on so warm a day?''

''I'll certainly carry this in for you,'' he said, taking up the basket again.

Valentina thanked him and tripped up the steps to
open the front door. Sir Derwent's eyes were frankly
admiring. It was rather nice to be looked at in such a
way again. She snatched off her apron, and invited
him to be seated while she arranged for refreshments
to be brought.

''I regret that I can stay but a moment, Miss Ashford.'' He put the laundry basket on a chest and

waited politely until Valentina had sat down, then settled himself on the faded blue sofa. His eyes flickered around the withdrawing room with a troubled expression. "May I ask if your brother is—er, an adult?"

"He is. Are you perhaps so kind as to be concerned for our safety?"

"And with good reason, ma'am." His face suddenly grim, he said, "Egad, but I'd not have believed even de Michel would allow his kinfolks to dwell in such a pigsty."

Valentina's smile faded. "You are acquainted with my cousin, Sir Derwent?"

For a moment he did not answer, staring down at the hat in his hand. Then, he said in a low voice, "To my sorrow, ma'am. I know him for a traitor to his country, a rogue and a blackguard! I would not trust any woman within a mile of him unless she went protected by several armed guards!"

Valentina said coldly, "I think you forget yourself! Charles de Michel is my kinsman, and I dwell here only by his kindness. I must ask that you not—"

"Not speak the truth?" His mouth twisted, and he said bitterly, "Do you fancy any gentleman would thus blacken another man's character without cause? It is easy to see that despite your present circumstances you are gently born and likely have no conception of the evil you risk."

Frowning, Valentina came to her feet. Locks stood at once, but gave her no opportunity to speak, saying, "You need not ask me to leave—I am going. But

I cannot in good conscience go without I warn you. I implore you, if it is humanly possible, leave this house of infamy before you are judged to be as vile as he. If he has you so trapped you cannot escape, then keep a pistol always within reach. May God keep and protect you, Miss Ashford." And with a wild gesture somewhere between a wave and a benediction, he was gone.

"By all the saints," cried Lady Clara, hurrying in with flour on the end of her nose, "who was that distracted creature?"

Following her, stripping off his gauntlets, Ashford said, "Are you all right, Tina? I vow I've only to turn my back for an instant and the curst place is overrun with Bedlamites!"

Valentina held out the calling card. "Did you both hear him then? The man is positively eaten up with hatred!"

"Never heard of the birdwit." Ashford passed the card to his aunt. "We heard his last few sentences and came running. We were sure you entertained a madman."

"Aha . . ." said Lady Clara very softly. "So that is the way of it. Sir Derwent Locks' wife is the lady your cousin ran away with. He is the man Charles nigh killed in their duel. Though I fancy the only one knows the truth of the whole matter, is—"

"Leslie! Tina! Help me! Help!"

They were all running to the door even as the last word died into a sobbing wail.

"Lord above! Now what?" puffed my lady.

Muttering an oath, Ashford flung the door wide and sprang down the steps.

Following, Valentina gave a gasp of horror.

Her eyes red and swollen, her flushed face streaked with tears, her hair a tumbled wreck, Sidonie tottered to her brother's arms. Behind her came Charles de Michel, riding FitzMoke. And Mr. de Michel's hair was dishevelled and his face marked by long scratches.

"Thank ... God! I am safe now...." moaned Sidonie.

Pale with wrath, Ashford demanded, "What the devil have you done to her?"

"Raped her," answered de Michel with acerbity. "What would you expect?"

CHAPTER THREE

VALENTINA GAVE A GASP OF RAGE. Sidonie shrieked. Ashford swore ringingly, thrust his sister into his aunt's arms and sprinted into the house.

"For shame, sir!" cried Valentina.

"Leslie! Wh-where's Leslie g-gone...?" sobbed Sidonie.

"To get his pistol of course, you silly chit," growled de Michel, dismounting and limping to face the hostile little group.

"Oh! Oh! Oh!" she cried at full volume. "He'll kill you!"

"And if he does it will be your own fault, nephew," declared Lady Clara. "What a disgraceful thing to say in front of ladies."

He shrugged. "I am a disgraceful—and much tried man. But if I offended you, I apologize. You may set it down to vexation. It was very obviously the scenario Ashford had painted for himself and after what I had endured I was in no mood for more nonsense." He met Sidonie's great terrified eyes and added contemptuously, "Have no fears, little watering pot. I could out-shoot your noble brother with my eyes closed."

"And leave him...d-dead at your horrid...feet," said Sidonie between sobs.

"Then you had best not have set up your silly yowling to be rescued, but rather have told him the truth."

Well acquainted with her sister's love of drama, Valentina met her aunt's uneasy glance with one as dubious. "It might be nice if someone would explain all this," she said. "Exactly what—"

"Stand away from that filthy libertine," roared Ashford from the top of the steps, looking very dashingly all fire and fury and with his horse pistol levelled at de Michel.

"Scene Two of the Ashford Family Farce," muttered de Michel, disgusted.

Sidonie threw herself between them, arms flung out to the sides. "He has done nothing, dearest brother," she declared in a voice that could be heard in the stables.

"Not so loud, Sarah Siddons." A twinkle crept into de Michel's eyes. "You'll ruin my reputation."

Frowning at his youngest sister, Ashford hesitated. "Then why were you in such a state?" He turned on de Michel. "Sir, I demand to know what happened between you!"

"Demand away. I'll explain nothing with that thing pointing at me, though I doubt you know how to shoot.

Ashford said hotly, "You may believe I do! I'm a dashed good marksman!"

"Hah! Typical of youth. All show and no go. I'll warrant you couldn't even knock off that red rose."

"Then you'd lose, damn your eyes!" Ashford took careful aim at the rose and fired. Aunt Clara and Sidonie held their ears as the shot resounded. The rose disintegrated. De Michel glanced at Valentina, saw laughter in her eyes and for an instant stared at her rather blankly. Then he said, "Jolly good shot, Ashford. Now we know your pistol's not loaded, don't we?"

"Oh—Egad," mumbled Ashford, flushing scarlet.

De Michel slipped a small but deadly-looking weapon from his pocket. "Were I of a mind to use this, now..."

Sidonie howled, "Do not! For mercy's sake! Do not!"

"Good Lord!" De Michel eyed her with revulsion and replaced the pistol. "Never fall for a trick like that again, else your skill will avail you nought, my lad."

"Meanwhile," said Lady Clara, "I suggest we take this drama inside. You appear to have come to grief, de Michel."

He gave her his rare smile. "Thank you, Lady Aunt, but I'll get on my way."

"I still want to know what happened," persisted Ashford doggedly.

"Ask your tragedienne," said de Michel. "She will make the tale far more entertaining than could I."

Clara led the wilting Sidonie into the house, Ashford holding his sister's other arm, glad to escape the mockery in de Michel's eyes.

Valentina said quietly, "You have a wicked tongue, but I rather suspect we owe you an apology, cousin. It's a long walk home. Would you care to ride Ashford's horse? Or we could harness our cob to the donkey cart."

"Not at all necessary, ma'am. My friend FitzMoke won't mind."

Watching him limp towards the patient little animal, Valentina asked, "Is your ankle sprained, do you think?"

"Oh, I rather doubt it. Just a twist." He mounted up with no sign of discomfort, then turned FitzMoke and rode back to her. "I'd intended to inspect your progress, Miss Valentina. Thanks to the machinations of your sister you've won a day's grace."

She dropped a small curtsey. "You are all that is conciliating, sir."

"To the contrary, I am a hard, cruel, and depraved traitor, as anyone will gladly inform you. I'll own myself puzzled on one score, however. It appears that your father bred *you* up properly. And your brother will be a good enough man when he's had some of the edges rubbed off. Why did no one take your sister in hand? Her selfishness and vanity bear off the palm!"

"And your arrogance bears off a whole palm tree!" flared Valentina.

"Oh yes. But that is an evasion, m'dear coz."

The grin hovered about his mouth again. Disconcerted by it, Valentina said frowningly, "Sidonie was very frail as a child. We—we may perhaps have indulged her a trifle, but—"

"A trifle!"

"But she can be warm and loving and—"

"She is *still* a child, playing children's games. But she has all the instincts of a siren, and the shape and looks to match. She's not the sense to realize she plays with fire. If you had your wits about you, she'd not be let out of your sight without a reliable companion!"

Valentina opened her mouth to retaliate, then closed it again.

The donkey ambled away, de Michel sitting straight enough, his long legs hanging down on each side of the small animal.

Disturbed, Valentina went into the house.

The family had gathered in the withdrawing room, Sidonie seated on the sofa with Ashford's arm still around her. The girl was weeping miserably, and Aunt Clara was evidently concluding a stern homily.

"...not only foolish but might well have involved your brother in a duel which would, I am persuaded, have been needless and could have had tragic consequences."

"I s-said I am s-sorry." Sidonie dabbed at her reddened eyes. "All I did was to—to go for a little walk, and—"

"Which of itself was most improper. You are a young lady, and—"

"In London I was a young lady," interrupted the girl, hysteria again creeping into her voice. "Here—what am I? A country d-drudge!"

"Yes, we know love," said Ashford, patting her shoulder kindly. "None of us like it."

"Valentina likes it," gulped Sidonie. "And she likes—*him!* She d-doesn't care how he—insulted me!"

"I like living in the country, I'll own," said Valentina, a little flushed. "But you cannot think I like having to work so hard, dearest. And as for Mr. de

Michel, I don't like most of the things I hear about him. I take it you met him on your walk?''

"I'm tired," declared Sidonie, drying her tears and pouting. "I don't want to talk about it."

"Well you must talk about it, child," said Lady Clara, unfamiliarly stern. "You have impugned the honour of a gentleman, and—"

"Hah!"

"And endangered your brother's life. Charles de Michel is a very dangerous man and a dead shot. Nonetheless, if he really did insult you, Ashford must call him to account. I am going to put you on your honour, Sidonie, to answer truthfully. Now—what did the man do to you?"

Sidonie looked around, and seeing three grave faces, was frightened. "He set his horse to ride me down."

"Good heavens," gasped Valentina. "Were you running away, then?"

"Well, I started to, but when I sat up—"

"Sat up?" echoed Lady Clara incredulous. "You were lying down?"

Sidonie bit her lip. "It was hot, and—and I had walked so far—not realizing it, of course. So I just lay down for a minute."

"On the *road*?" said Ashford, his brows lowering.

"No, of course not silly. Under a tree."

Valentina frowned. "Do you say that de Michel was so foolish as to gallop his horse among trees?"

"Er—well, I wasn't quite *under* the trees. It was so nice and sunny, you know." Condemnation was dawning in their faces, and Sidonie rushed on, "He said he didn't see me, but—"

"Of course he didn't see you," broke in Ashford. "That gown is green, and likely blended with the grass. Besides, who would expect to see a lady sleeping all alone in the fields? Good Lord, Sid! How could you be such a widgeon? If that's all he did—"

"Of course it's not all he did! He swore and bellowed like—like a pirate, as if I'd *mean't* that he should be thrown!"

Ashford grinned suddenly. "What did you do? Jump up at the last minute and shriek at him, and off he popped? Gad, but I'd like to have seen it!"

"I did not shriek at him! I tried very hard in fact to be pleasant." Sidonie smiled reminiscently. "I was all gentle femininity, soft and clinging, and—"

Correctly reading her brother's expression, Valentina inserted swiftly, "I wonder so hot-blooded a man could resist you, dearest."

"Hot-blooded?" Sidonie's rapt expression faded into indignation. "He is as cold as any fish! He looked down at me—"

Ashford inserted, "I thought you said you jumped up."

"Well, I did but I chanced to sort of—fall against him."

Lady Clara gave a knowing grunt. "Half-fainting, and adorably helpless, eh, you little rascal? So he looked down at you, and...?"

"And for a minute I thought—" Sidonie tossed her head. "But he is an utter boor. 'Don't!' he says. And when I asked what he meant, he snarled like a veritable ogre, 'Don't flirt.' And he said—" her eyes flashed with wrath ''—he said he was no—no *nursery Lothario!*''

Her three hearers promptly lapsed into whoops of laughter.

''Oho!'' howled Ashford. ''No nursery—Lothario! Egad, what a set-down!''

''P-Poor de Michel,'' wheezed Aunt Clara, holding her sides. ''And—and then for you nephew, to name him a filthy libertine! Oh, my stars!''

Sidonie stamped her foot. ''Go on, laugh, all of you,'' she raged. ''I suppose you care nothing for the fact that the loathsome reptile made me walk all the way home, while he rode that ugly little donkey!''

''Now dearest,'' said Valentina breathlessly. ''You can scarce blame him for that. After all, he was unhorsed, and made to look very foolish.''

''Yes,'' agreed Sidonie, somewhat mollified. ''And he wrenched his ankle, and his hand bled all over his pretty grey—er, unmentionables. Which he richly deserved, the beast.''

The smile faded from Valentina's eyes.

Lady Clara said sharply, ''And none of it would have happened had you not behaved improperly from start to finish, miss!''

''Don't pout, Sid,'' put in Ashford, taking her hand. ''You must be a good sportsman, you know.''

They all thought she was to blame, she could see it. Because he had extended his miserable mite of charity they would not see that Charles de Michel had shamed her. Well, someday—somehow, she would even the score, and it would be Sidonie Margaret Ashford who would have the last laugh!

She smiled. "Yes—you're right of course," she
said.

THE CLOTHES-LINE had blown down while they had
their family conference. By the time they'd discovered the disaster, Mandarin had pursued an exploring
cat among the trailing and still damp articles wherefore the following day Valentina was doomed to scullery and scrubbing board again. This was worrying,
for she had hoped to work in the book room, which
had not even been dusted as yet. They had originally
decided to spend one week on each floor of the house,
and since the cellar and second floor were each
roughly half the size of the ground and first floors,
such things as window cleaning, and weeding the immediately adjacent flower-beds could, they'd confidently anticipated, occupy the fourth week of their
allotted month. The thing they'd failed to take into
account was the simple business of existing while the
work went forward. Shopping for food and supplies,
preparing meals, washing up afterwards, all took so
much longer than any of them had anticipated. And
as for the laundry! Valentina sighed and blew away a
stray lock of hair that persisted in curling around her
nose.

It was hot, and her back was beginning to ache. This
miserable sheet was being deliberately uncooperative,
and her hands, which were quite strong, seemed unable to wring as effectively as they should. Horace was
outside, pounding on the recalcitrant pump, and between the heat and his hammer-blows she had a nasty
headache. Succeeding in wringing out the hot soapy

water at last, or so much of it as she could manage, she dumped the sheet into the big tub of rinse water. Promptly, a retaliatory wave sloshed down the front of her, soaking both the towel she'd tied around her small waist, and her pale orange batiste gown. "Oh, confound you," she moaned.

"What—oaths from a lady?" Poised and elegant, Charles de Michel was beside her. He wore a dark grey coat of Bath suiting, his cravat was a masterpiece in which a diamond pin blazed, his waistcoat was primrose, his unmentionables pale pearly grey, and his boots so bright they fairly dazzled. Having a fair estimation of her own bedraggled appearance, Valentina could have sunk, and her mortification was not improved when he raised a jewelled quizzing glance and scanned her from head to toe.

"The ultimate unkindness, cousin," she told him with a wry smile.

The quizzing glass lifted to the level of her eyes. A faint frown replaced his look of amusement. "Why do you struggle with this alone? Each time I come, you seem to be bearing the lion's share of the work. Where is that fine brother of yours?"

"He went to see you and apologize."

"And accomplished it quite well. I'd fancied he meant to come straight here and take his share of the work."

"Ashford has worked very hard indeed." Valentina lifted the soaked apron to wipe soapsuds from her chin. "You will see how much he's accomplished."

"From what I've seen thus far," he said, still frowning at her, "it is far from being enough. You are shockingly behind schedule, ma'am."

"We are quite aware of our time limits," said Valentina frigidly. "Unfortunately, everyday needs must be met also."

"Is that what your aunt and the darling of Drury Lane are about?"

Valentina's chin lifted, soapsuds and all. "If you refer to my sister, Mr. de Michel, she is picking peas for our dinner. There are some vines behind the house in what is left of the vegetable garden. Lady Clara is in the barn—she believes Mandarin chased a cat in there last evening, and is afraid the poor creature may have been injured."

"Dear me. I can see you will never meet my terms, Miss Valentina. I'll not further delay your labours, but will be about my tour of inspection."

He limped out, leaving Valentina angrier than ever as she began to wring the rinse water from her sheet. The mangle was old, and to maneouvre the sheet through the rollers was an art she could not seem to master. She struggled mightily, dreading that the horridly bulky article might drag on the floor and dirty itself again. She was well-soaked by the time she succeeded in getting a wedge of sheet between the rollers, but to guide the balance while she turned the handle seemed beyond her ability, however she struggled.

"What a fuss you make over so simple a thing!" De Michel was beside her again. "That's not the way to do it."

At the end of her endurance, Valentina jerked her head up. "Of all the odious...opinionated..." she panted, and stopped, because he was stripping off his coat.

"Stand back, madam," he said, "and allow your tyrannical landlord to show you how one plays this game."

"No, really cousin, you are so elegant, and—"

"And you are hot and tired and positively drooping," he finished briskly. "Never let it be said this libertine allowed a lady to wash herself to death! Your problem, Miss Tina, is that you are trying to push too much of a wodge through this—er device." He unwound rapidly.

Valentina gave a shriek and sprang forward, and between them they prevented the slithering sheet from reaching the floor.

"Er—yes," said de Michel, wet to the elbows. "Now, I will effect a neat fold...so..." Concentrating, he glanced up, saw her anxiety, and his lips twitched into something suspiciously like a grin. "*Voilà!* Simplicity itself when approached scientifically. Do you hold that end whilst I demonstrate the function of this—er—"

"Mangle," supplied Valentina. "Pray *do* be careful, cousin!"

He lifted one hand and said grandly, "Observe and learn, madam!"

Guiding the dripping sheet with his left hand, he bent forward, turning smoothly. "All the wails about washday are nonsense. If females would but take the trouble to be organized they'd find most tasks per-

fectly simple. Are you catching it at the back? I—''
The word ended in a squawk as he jerked his head up
and then down again.

"Can you not get the last bit through?" Valentina
came quickly to assist him to turn the handle.

"Help...!" croaked de Michel, cheek to sheet.

Bewildered, she peered at him. "What...on
earth...? Charles—stand up straight!"

"Can...not."

"Oh my heavens! You have hurt your back!" She
seized the handle again. "I'll wind the rest of this—''

"No!" he screeched. "You're—strangling...
me!"

Mystified, she stooped to peer at his convulsed face.

Bent double, he gave her a ghastly grin. "Un...
wind."

Beginning to comprehend, she wound the handle
backwards.

The sheet, a red-faced de Michel, and the black
ribbon of his quizzing glass came into view.

"Oh...my...goodness," gulped Valentina, trying
not to laugh.

With an ominous crunching, the quizzing glass itself appeared, considerably bent.

De Michel held up the shattered remains, then raised
dejected eyes to Valentina. Both hands clapped over
her mouth, she was convulsed, tears of mirth beginning to flow down her cheeks.

"What in the name of..." Ashford paused in the
scullery door, staring from his drenched sister to his
almost equally drenched cousin.

"I'll tell you what it is," said de Michel, ignoring Valentina's wails as he took up his coat. "Your sister wants for a proper sense of gratitude! I was good enough—" he was obliged to raise his voice "—to try and help her, and—" He shook the wreckage of the quizzing glass under Ashford's nose. "I incline to the belief, coz, that your family is an unmitigated disaster!"

He made his haughty way to the door, then turned a stern countenance. "When you are done laughing at my discomfiture, madam, you had best be careful—there is glass in that sheet!"

Coming into the scullery a few minutes later, Lady Clara said, "The cat has had six kittens, Tina. The dearest little— Goodness gracious, what a mess! Is this what Cousin Charles was laughing at? I could hear him all the way down the drivepath!"

THE EVENING WAS SULTRY, the eastern horizon lit with occasional flashes of lightning. Sidonie and Ashford played dominoes after dinner, then took Mandarin for a walk. Sharing a branch of candles with her aunt as they sat mending, Valentina chuckled softly.

Lady Clara smiled at her, "You are thinking of your cousin again."

"Oh, Aunt, if only you had been here!"

"As well I wasn't. Had I seen *her* son condescending to turn a mangle, I'd have been properly bowled out!"

Valentina glanced at her curiously. "You never did finish telling me about it, dear. Why do you so dislike Aunt Ruth?"

"It would be un-Christian to say." My lady stabbed her needle into the heel of the sock she was mending and set Christianity aside. "Save that because she is pretty she fancies the universe was created only for her! You likely think me a jealous old woman, but—"

"I think it is going to rain," said Ashford, ushering his sister into the room. "We saw the kittens. Like so many drowned rats."

"They are adorable." With a sidelong glance at the pile of mending Sidonie added, "There's a storm some way off, and it has given me the headache, so I think I'll go early to bed."

"Poor dear," said Valentina. "Is it one of your bad ones?"

"Not yet." Sidonie kissed her goodnight. "Sleep well, darling."

Lady Clara yawned, and put down her darning. "My eyes are too tired. I think I'll come up with you, love." She said her goodnights and started off. "Where is Mandy?"

Settling himself into a chair with a copy of yesterday's *Times*, Ashford answered, "He wouldn't come in. Too warm, I expect. The kittens are safe enough, though. I put their box up on the work-bench."

Valentina promised to fetch the dog in when she came to bed, and resumed her mending, busied with her thoughts, listening with only half an ear to what Ashford read from the newspaper.

"They've built another of those railway engine things. This one's called the *Puffing Billy*. Gad but I'd like to see it!"

"I would be scared to death!" ('He took it in very good part, for such a proud young man. How his eyes light up when he smiles. I wonder if he really is a Bonapartist....')

"This writer says Wellington is to be criticized because he is making haste slowly for the Pyrenees. Jupiter! Are they never satisfied? His lordship has done splendidly."

"Oh, very true, love. Splendidly." ('I wonder if he loved Lady Locks. He doesn't seem to be with her now. Perhaps he is betrothed to another lady. I hadn't noticed that he has a cleft in his chin.')

"...And what I wouldn't give to be with them!" Ashford folded the paper with a slam, tossed it aside, and sat gnawing his knuckles broodingly.

'He is in one of his bitter moods, poor boy.' Returning to the here and now, Valentina asked, "Be with whom, love? Oh—in Spain, do you mean?"

"His lordship won't be in Spain for long. I'll wager he'll have crossed the frontier before this year is out! I should be doing something for my country. But here I sit. Tidying an old house like—like a woman!"

Valentina put down her mending. "I know how hard it is for you, but—"

"Hard! It's a curst cage!" He sprang up and began to pace about distractedly. "I was sure Great-Uncle Silas could get me that naval appointment! If you knew how I *counted* on it, Tina! But he did—nothing!"

"I'm sure the old gentleman tried. Perhaps he could not."

"That's very obvious, isn't it? And I've not the funds to buy a pair of colours. What's ahead? What in the devil am I to do with my life? Deteriorate into a bucolic farmer? Spend the rest of my days perched on the side of that damned quarry with de Michel?"

Intrigued, she asked, "Whatever do you mean?"

He gave a scornful snort. "Didn't you know? He has some tomfool notion to make it into a garden. A *garden!* That ugly, bare great red hole in the ground! The fellow's mad! When I went over to apologize to him this morning, he told me that if we finish with this monstrosity in time, I can help him! *Par grace!*"

How desperate he looked. She said gently, "Poor darling. This is miserable for you, I know."

He swung around and came at once to kneel beside her chair and take her hand. "What a wretch I am to grumble, when you have been so good. All I think of is myself while my poor sister's eyes are so red and tired. You've been hard at it since dawn, I'll wager!"

She chuckled. "Not quite that long. And it is not so vexing for me because to an extent Sid was right. I do like the country. That doesn't make it any easier for you, alas, but this bad time will pass, I know it. Perhaps Cousin Charles can be persuaded to buy you a cornetcy, if you have decided you want an hussar regiment. But I'd thought it was Navy or nothing?"

"It was. But I don't care now. Anything! *Anything* rather than this utter boredom." He bowed his curly head against her sleeve. "If only I could find a way to provide for you girls, I'd join up. By God, but I would!"

"Leslie! The rank and file? Whatever would poor Papa think?"

"I know, I know." He came to his feet and looked down at her, trying not very successfully to smile. "I'm an ungrateful block." He bent and kissed her. "Forgive me, Tina."

She caressed his cheek. "There is nothing to forgive. You're young and full of hopes and dreams and spirit. Naturally, you want to be striving and achieving—climbing your mountains wherever or whatever they be. You'd not be much of a man, else. Just be patient a little longer, dear. Something will happen—I know it!"

She was thinking of those brave words half an hour later when she went onto the steps to call Mandarin. The storm had blown away, but the night was quite wild, with a warm wind sending cloud wrack scurrying across the three-quarter moon. Valentina called, but there came no scamper of busy feet or the snuffling little barks with which the Pekingese usually answered a summons.

There was no sign of him in the gardens nor the barn and stables. Irritated, Valentina began to walk down the drivepath. Aunt Clara doted on the pompous little creature, and if he had wandered off and got himself lost the dear lady would be devastated. It was by now well past her bedtime, and she was tired, but she went on, calling and searching for him, her anxiety increasing with each moment. Not until she found herself at the top of the hill, looking down on the steward's cottage did she realize how far she had come. She was shocked. Only yesterday she had

scolded her sister for walking out alone in the day-
time, and here she was, all alone and far from home
at almost twelve o'clock midnight! And—good heavens!—The Galloping Gent had been active on these
roads for some time and had struck not five miles
away only two nights since! Mandarin or no, she must
get home at once.

Turning about, she felt scared suddenly, and the
shadowy lane, which had seemed only a pleasant
country by-way on the way up the hill, became a sin-
ister and threatening chasm on the way down. Keeping to the shade of the hedgerows she walked quickly,
but halted as there came a rapid tattoo of hoofbeats.
It did not even occur to her panicked mind that this
might be some innocent citizen upon a perfectly
harmless errand. She shrank deeper into the shadow
of the hedge and waited, scarcely daring to breathe.

The rider was almost upon her. A consummate
horseman, he leaned forward in the saddle, the cape
of his riding coat flying with the speed of that thundering gallop. He passed by so closely that Valentina
felt she could have stretched out a hand and touched
the big black horse. She saw the rider clearly. His hat
was tilted at a jaunty angle, his eyes narrowed, his lean
face set in a mask of rage made grimmer by the wild
untidiness of the dark windblown hair. It was Charles
de Michel.

CHAPTER FOUR

"WELL, WELL," drawled de Michel. "We have caught a bookworm in the act, my dear Stane."

Curled up on the floor, leaning against the shelves she was supposed to be dusting, Sidonie dropped the volume of engravings she had been leafing through, and looked up in comical dismay.

The large young gentleman with the flaming red hair bent to extend a hand and assist her to her feet, admiration in his honest blue eyes.

"Miss Industry—I mean, Miss Sidonie Ashford," said de Michel. "Lord Samuel Stane, cousin."

Sidonie darted a malevolent glare at de Michel, then turned a melting glance on the husky young giant beside him. "How do you do, my lord?" She dropped him a curtsy, all demure and youthful loveliness despite her plain round gown.

He bowed. "Your servant, ma'am."

"Perhaps we might interrupt your—er, labours long enough for you to fetch your sister," said de Michel.

Her little hands clenched; for a minute he thought she would fly out at him, then she pressed dainty fingers to her cheek, looked up at Lord Stane despairingly, and fled, head bent and a realistic sob echoing behind her.

His eyes slightly dazed, his lordship said, "A bit hard on her, weren't you, Charles? She's little more than a child, after all, and—"

"A child tigress!" De Michel tapped his friend on the shoulder with the riding crop he carried. "'Ware, Sam. She'd eat you alive."

The "tigress" in question looked more like an angry kitten as she flounced into the scullery where Valentina was ironing one of Ashford's shirts. "Prepare thyself, beggar maid," she warned. "The Dirty Frog awaits you in the book room, and is as rude and horrid as ever."

Valentina stood the iron on its heel and stared at her. "Do you refer to our benefactor, by any chance?"

"I refer to Charles de Michel," answered Sidonie, her lower lip pouting. "Never look so holier than thou, Tina! Everyone knows he is half-French by birth, and all French by inclination! I dare not guess how many of our brave men he has betrayed to their deaths, or—"

"That—will—do!" Valentina's eyes blazed. "To call Cousin Charles names is not only childish but in very bad taste since we live under his protection. To make such irresponsible and deadly accusations with only your dislike of him as justification is disgraceful! For shame, Sidonie!" She swept out, leaving her sister gazing after her in genuine dismay.

This time Valentina remembered to take off her apron and mob-cap and pat her hair into some semblance of tidiness before she entered the book room. De Michel, informally clad in riding dress, was limping about, accompanied by a young gentleman whose shoulders seemed likely to burst the seams of his bottle green coat. When de Michel introduced his lordship, Stane took Valentina's fingertips as if they were fashioned from thin crystal and the shy smile he gave her won her liking immediately.

"I brought a friend to protect me." De Michel's dark eyes quizzed her. "Since I seem always to come to grief when I am in your vicinity."

Valentina glanced up the length of Lord Stane and remarked that her cousin had chosen well.

Stane flushed with pleasure, especially since Miss Sidonie had come quietly into the room and stood just inside the door with a chastened look on her lovely face. "I think it unlikely Charles would need—or even wish—to be protected against such charming ladies as yourselves."

"His fears are unfounded," said Valentina. "We've woven no evil spells against him." She added thoughtfully, "As yet."

De Michel smiled. "You terrify me, ma'am. Ashford, I think you know Stane."

Looking hot and grimy, and with a small ladder under one arm, Ashford came into the room and nodded to his lordship.

"I'm glad you're here," went on de Michel. "I have been making an inspection tour, and considering that there are three ladies and two men engaged in this venture, your progress seems markedly slow. If you all are applying yourselves industriously, I'd think you might have reached the first floor by now, instead of which—" he ran one finger along a bookshelf, and shook his head "—you've not even dusted in here."

"What the deuce d'you think we are?" blazed Ashford. "A parcel of damned navvies? My aunt and my sisters are ladies of Quality."

"Are you saying you wish to cancel our bargain?" enquired de Michel with the bored lift of one eyebrow.

"If it was up to me—" Ashford paused helplessly.

De Michel tapped the handle of his riding crop against his chin. "You fancy this work demeaning, do you? Rather be on the strut in St. James's, eh?"

Ashford flushed.

"Leslie had hoped to be commissioned to the Navy," said Valentina, quick to resent any criticism of her brother.

"Why?" asked de Michel, without interest. "Have we a wish to see the world? Or is this a patriot's zeal to strike a blow for king and country?"

Ashford flared hotly, "I hope I may be judged a patriot. And I'd like to see some action, 'pon my soul but I would! There's precious little to be had around here!"

"Not so little," put in Stane with his pleasant smile. "Last night our local member of the High Toby struck again."

De Michel said, "What—The Galloping Gent? They'll be putting a price on his head at this rate. Who did he hold up this time, Sam?"

"Locks." His lordship looked grave. "He was robbed of a fat purse, and other valuables. To add insult to injury, the highwayman informed him he had a foul mouth and when Locks raved on, disregarding the fact that there was a lady at his side, the fellow challenged him to a duel there and then!''

"Oh! How romantic!'' gasped Sidonie, her great eyes aglow.

"How stupid rather,'' said de Michel. "The silly block could well have been apprehended while he dallied about. Besides, Locks is a fine shot. The Galloping Gent would likely have had his head blown off for his bravado.''

"Well, he didn't,'' his friend contradicted. "They did fight, and The Gent is evidently a superb marksman. He blew Locks' pistol right out of his hand, stole a kiss from his lady, and left him raving.''

Sidonie squealed and gave a little jump, clapping her hands with delight.

De Michel murmured, "How fortunate I did not stir abroad last night, else dear Derwent would most assuredly have said I was the dastardly rank rider. Where did you cull all this news, Sam?''

"At *The Sow's Ear*. Locks' man was in the yard this morning and the inn fairly buzzed with the tale.''

"Then I must go at once and relay the news to my mama and convince her the country is not so devoid of excitement as she believes.'' With a bow to the two girls and the murmured suggestion that they not waste any more time, de Michel conducted his reluctant friend from the house.

"Not waste our time, indeed,'' muttered Ashford, glaring after his departing figure. "I'd like to know how he spends *his* time!''

"Worshipping Napoleon Bonaparte,'' said Sidonie. "Oh, I'm sorry, Tina. But did you see how he looked at me? One might suppose me to be an infant!''

"I saw how Lord Stane looked at you," said Valentina, attempting to pour oil on troubled waters.

Ashford grinned. "So did I. You've made another conquest, Sid."

The beauty shrugged her shoulders. "That great silly creature?" She retrieved her duster, saying thoughtfully, "Still, he *is* a peer..." Glancing mischievously at Valentina she encountered a stern look, and went at once to take her sister's hand and peer up into her face. "Are you still vexed with me, dearest? I'm naughty, I know, but I promise to work like two Amazons and never call him The Dirty Frog again if you will but forgive me."

Valentina kissed her, and wished de Michel might have seen the sweet, penitent little face. But going in search of Aunt Clara she thought, 'He *was* out last night! Why should he lie about it?'

IT WAS A BRILLIANT MORNING. Yesterday's mugginess had been blown away, the air was bracing, and the few clouds were small powder puffs against the cornflower blue of the skies. Deep in thought, de Michel saw none of the beauties surrounding them, and Lord Stane respected his silence. The horses trotted along the sun-dappled lane, the birds sang, and all was peaceful. A deceptive peace, thought Stane, and glanced at de Michel again.

"Conscience, Charles?"

"Devil a bit of it! I allow them to live in my house. Why should I be conscience-stricken if—they..." The haughty words faltered to a stop. "Blast you, Sam," he said with a wry grin. "You know me too well."

Stane chuckled. "Then why do a good deed with a scowl and make them hate you for it, when you might do it with a smile and—"

"And make them—what? Love me? Hah!"

Stane said earnestly, "You are your own worst enemy. You consistently play your cards all wrong, and now you're at it again. One catches more flies with honey than with vinegar, my friend."

For a long moment de Michel did not reply. Then he said with a slow smile, "What fustian you do talk. I played the cards as they were dealt. I've many reasons for not wanting the Ashfords here. Miss Valentina forced them on me, and I gave her no more than she deserved. Only..." Another pause, then he muttered almost to himself, "Our would-be Admiral's sister has spunk to match her beauty."

"She is exquisite," his lordship agreed. "When she jumped up and down, did you mark her dainty little feet?"

De Michel grinned. "Gudgeon," he said. "You have everything hind end foremost, as usual!"

"HE IS A VERY SMALL DOG," said Valentina, fingering the bolt of pale green velvet and thinking how well it would look on Sidonie.

Mrs. Bellewood, the proprietor of the only millinery shop in Wye Dilly, thought that you could always spot a lady of Quality, even if her dark blue tunic was a little frayed here and there and the paler blue of the India muslin gown beneath it was somewhat faded.

"He's not been seen in the village, Miss Ashford," she said in her positive fashion, "or I'd have heard of't. Had him a long time, has ye? Likely fond o' the little chap. A body can get right fond o' dogs, fer all they be a nuisance."

"Lady Rustwick is extreme fond of Mandarin," said Valentina. "She has been out all day, calling to him. I was hopeful he might have wandered this way. If he should do so, perhaps you would be good enough to keep him here and send word to us."

Through the open door she saw de Michel limping along the street. He was a far cry from the elegant young gentleman who had called at the Towers this morning. His coat was shabby, his boots dulled, his neckcloth all askew, and the dark hair even more rumpled and untidy about his hatless head.

"*Amos!*" Mrs. Bellewood's voice was a window-shattering howl. "The *master's* come! Best step lively!"

'Good gracious,' thought Valentina. 'Is everyone afraid of the man?'

As if to deny her thought, a grubby small boy ran up the street, seized de Michel's hand and jumped along with him, grinning radiantly up into the dark face. Valentina held her breath. Surely her brusque cousin or cousin-once-removed or whatever he was, would not snub the child—he looked such a dear little boy. Her skirts rippled as a miniature tornado whizzed past, pulling on a nankeen jacket, inside out. "Wait fer me, Mr. Charles! Do wait fer me!" One yard of vibrant boy erupted onto the outer step and galloped along, knees flying. Astonished, Valentina went outside.

Where they all came from, she could not tell, but suddenly de Michel was at the centre of an uproarious and exuberant crowd of children. Boys and girls of all shapes, sizes, and ages, danced and jumped and ran, like so many pins to the dark young man's magnet, while he grinned and nodded and managed to get in a word here and there, his remarks usually eliciting shrieks of laughter. Valentina heard snatches of the repartee: "...My turn to bowl first!... Be on Bill's team, sir?... But you promithed I could bat thith time, Mithter Charleth!" (this from a diminutive damsel with many freckles and a dress several sizes too large so that she constantly tripped over the hem.)

Valentina blinked at Mrs. Bellewood, who had followed her onto the step.

"Rounders," said that dame succinctly.

"Ah. So that's why they flock around him."

The large lady chuckled. "Lord love ye, no ma'am. It don't make no never-mind. They wait fer Friday afternoons, sartin-surely. But it be the same whenever Mr. Charles do come, whether it be to see about repairs on a cottage or old Perce's sow—to see the sow I mean, not to repair it!—or whatever. I dunno what there be about the master, but the children cannot keep away from him, and that's the truth of it!"

Baffled, Valentina thought, 'It doesn't fit the picture.'

A small hand tugged at her skirt.

"You are to come pleath, mith." The child with the too-large frock sent a hopeful beam up at her which betrayed the loss of two front teeth. "We haven't got enough umpireth and Mithter Charleth thayth you'll do."

Valentina had thought he'd not even seen her. "If that isn't just like—" she began indignantly. The beam faded from the bright little face. The child stepped back with a frightened look. "I'll have you know," said Valentina, hurriedly mending her fences, "that I am an excellent umpire!"

Casting a long-suffering glance at Mrs. Bellewood, who was all smiling approval, she allowed herself to be pulled to the village green where de Michel was already supervising the positioning of "posts" by means of sacks filled with sand.

"Umpire Ashford reporting, your worship," said Valentina.

"Right," he said, not so much as glancing at her. "You'll be batter's umpire. You know what that means, I presume?"

"Of course. I'm to look out for balls that are too high or too low, and to watch second and third posts."

Hoots arose.

Sack in hand, de Michel straightened, and sighed. "No, Miss Valentina. You're right about the first part, but you watch the first and fourth post catchers, not second and third."

"And you mutht watch the bowler," cautioned the tiny girl knowledgeably.

De Michel smiled down at her. "Right you are, Jennie. Do you have it now, ma'am?"

"I have it," nodded Valentina firmly, and added *sotto voce*, "Does this constitute part of my duties, sir?"

He said blandly, "Time off for good behaviour. All right, teams! Take your places!"

The children scattered, except for the small Jennie, who promptly fell flat on her face.

"Oh, drat!" said de Michel, lifting her as shouts of impatience arose. "Take that silly thing off, Jennie. You can play in your petticoats."

"Certainly not!" exclaimed Valentina, shocked. "She is a young lady! Here, Jennie, we'll manage." She unfastened the sash of her tunic, tied it tightly around the child's tiny waist, and hoisted the trailing skirts. A cheer went up as Jennie trotted happily to the back stop and struggled to raise the bat.

"Good heavens," whispered Valentina. "Is that wee mite to be first batsman?"

"Of course," said de Michel, starting off. "She'll be too tired later. Please get to your post now." He whistled shrilly. "Carry on!"

VALENTINA SIPPED the cold lemonade, sighed with pleasure, and leaned back on the bench outside *The Sow's Ear*. The sun was lower in the sky, and a warm golden light bathed the village green, filtered through the leaves of the ancient oaks, and twinkled on the latticed windows of the inn. "How they cheered," she said musingly. She turned and caught de Michel looking away quickly. "How long have you been organizing the game for them?"

"Since the little varmints badgered me into it. I vow, what with one annoyance and another, my life's not my own. Especially, of late." He slanted an oblique glance at her. "Now why do you smile, ma'am? I'd think you must fairly ache with weariness after that rough-and-tumble."

"Oh, no. I am accustomed to hard work, you see."

Still watching her, he said slowly, "Yes. I fancy you must yearn to be back in Town."

"Do you?"

"Of course. All ladies love the balls and parties and entertainments. It is the height of their ambition to spend two-thirds of the day changing their raiment so as to attend the endless round of frivolities and fustian."

"Whereas lofty intellects such as yours, loathe the opera, the theatre, the musicales and soirées where one may find writers and wits, and—"

"Half-wits, more likely," he interjected scornfully. "Egad, Miss Umpire, if one goes to the opera one goes in the company of those who attend only to ogle the dancers, or see who in the audience is with whom, and which lady is wearing what. At the theatre it is often difficult to hear the actors say their lines, so noisy and rude are the patrons. And as for musicales! To cringe through two hours of scraping and off-key fiddles and vast, screeching sopranos—" He shuddered. "Purgatory!"

She laughed. "There is no pleasing the man! What of your famous White's Club, and Watier's and all the other hallowed male haunts?"

His face became cold and closed, and the charming gleam of mischief faded from the dark eyes. "The last time I dared step across White's sacrosanct threshold, cousin, I was politely—perhaps not so politely—asked to leave."

Watching the proud aristocratic features, Valentina said hurriedly, "Papa used to say the best places for talk and wit were hidden away. And my brother Lincoln was forever at an old tavern down by the river, called—oh dear, whatever was it? Something about the jolly ghosts, or..."

"*The Merry Spirits?* Jove, but he was right!" From an icy and unapproachable statue he came glowingly to life once more, the finely shaped lips curving into a smile. "The evenings I've whiled away at that disreputable old haunt! And the company! Actors, posturing and intoning in all their glory; poets and playwrights reading their latest creative works—and often very creative indeed! Musicians, artists, men of words and wit, in truth! You should have heard the singing, Miss Tina! Every fellow had some ballad that was his alone, and we all would shout for it whenever he chanced to be there, and then everyone would sing together till the rafters fairly rang." He sighed nostalgically. "Around the fire, of a winter's night, it was better than all your White's and Brooks', and Golden Spoons."

Valentina watched him through a small silence, amazed by this glimpse of a very different Charles de Michel, and feeling a pang of sympathy that he had made such a sad muddle of his life.

Close by, a meadowlark soared up with a whir of wings. Abruptly recalled to the present, de Michel said, "If your brother used to go there, I've likely seen him, and never even knew he was my cousin. Is he in England still?"

"He is fighting in Spain."

All the animation died from his face again. "Oh."

"I pray he will soon be home," said Valentina. "He is the very dearest boy, and, speaking of home, I must—" She interrupted herself. "Oh, my heavens! I had quite forgot about poor Mandarin!"

"Mandarin?"

"My aunt's little dog. You saw him when first we moved in."

"I do seem to recall some demented creature. Why is he reduced to 'poor' Mandarin?"

"Because he wandered off yesterday evening, and has not come back. At least, he hadn't when I left today. Aunt Clara was distracted, and spent all morning searching the grounds and calling for him. That is why I walked into the village, in fact, to enquire if anyone had seen the poor little fellow. I *must* go, cousin. Pray excuse me."

"No, wait." He frowned, and muttered, "I wonder..."

Ten minutes later, de Michel slapped the reins on the mare's broad back and succeeded in rousing her to a trot. The donkey cart rattled and jolted, and Valentina clutched the side. Exasperated, de Michel said, "My apologies, Cousin Umpire. This racehorse is slowing down in her old age."

"Is she so old, then?"

"I think she mothered the charger of Alexander the Great! Only see how she plucks up her hocks! There's not a turtle alive could beat her! I should have asked you to wait whilst I sent someone for my curricle instead of hiring this hayburner from the inn."

"Never mind. We'll soon be there." Anxious, she said, "Do you really think Mandarin might have fallen into your quarry? Suppose he is killed! Aunt Clara will be devastated."

He clicked his tongue. "Supposition. A revolting pastime, ma'am. I'd thought you had more sense than to indulge such nonsense."

"You give me too much credit," she said, irked.

"Very true," he agreed maddeningly. "There is no end to it, you see. *Suppose* you do not finish your tasks at the Towers in time? *Suppose* your little sister runs off with Stane?—oh, I saw the look on his silly face this morning, as did you! *Suppose* I really am a dastardly Bonapartist? *Suppose* I am also The Galloping Gent?" Valentina gave a gasp, and he smiled his most cynical smile and added, "Yes, I saw that look, too."

She thought, 'He must have eyes in the back of his head!' And she said, "You do not miss very much, do you, cousin?"

"No. For instance, I take it you were the person I glimpsed skulking in the bushes last night."

"I was not skulking! I was looking for Mandarin."

"Were I your brother, ma'am, I'd soon put a stop to such clandestine idiocy! Respectable young females do not walk out alone after dark."

"I am far past my salad days. And I walk when and where I please."

"Well, if I catch you jauntering about at dead of night, Miss Ashford, you'll be taken home. Across my saddle bow, if necessary!" He saw the wrath in her expressive face and before she could voice her ire, swept on. "Aren't you going to ask me why I rode out last night and then denied it?"

Valentina had readied a cutting response to his insufferable male arrogance, and was caught off-stride. "No." She hesitated, trying to remember exactly how she had phrased her set-down, but instead said. "*Are* you The Galloping Gent?"

He threw back his head and laughed. "No beating about the bush for you, pretty cousin."

"Oh, how odious," she exclaimed. "I believe you said all those horrid things purely to aggravate me!"

"You aggravate most deliciously," he said, his eyes twinkling.

Valentina's confusion intensified. She knew her cheeks were red, and, furious with herself, could think of nothing to say.

"Here we are!" De Michel pulled up the mare, jumped from the cart, and reached up to lift Valentina down. With his strong hands about her waist she felt even more nervous and fluttery. She put both her own hands on his shoulders and for just a second he paused, holding her above him, smiling up at her. Then, "Don't hang about," he said severely, and set her down. "We must try to find your Chinese friend before the shadows become too deep."

They had stopped a short distance from the edge of the quarry. It was an ugly hole, stretching off for at least a quarter mile and being about two hundred yards across at its widest point. Only sparse turf and bushes grew near the rim, but the surrounding ground had been cleared of weeds, and there were evidences that the rough-hewn steps leading downwards had been restored and reinforced for part of the way. The balance of the descent was precipitous, with many of the steps missing altogether, and the remainder looking decidedly unsafe. Valentina trod nearer, and thought, 'What an ugly place! As if anyone could make a garden of this!'

A strong hand gripped her own. De Michel said, "Afraid of heights, are you? *Tu peux être tranquille, mademoiselle*. I have you fast."

With the strongest feeling that he was laughing at her, she responded a stately, *"Merci bien, monsieur,"* and ventured to the edge.

At the bottom, the ground stretched away in a mass of water-filled holes and uneven piles of red rock and debris. It looked a sullen and alien place, and she murmured anxiously, "Surely he would not have been so silly as to go down into that horrible great pit."

De Michel's grip tightened on her hand. He said, "Contrary to the popular myths, dogs are comparatively stupid creatures, ma'am. Your beloved Mandarin is likely no exception and went charging brainlessly where angels fear to tread."

"Mandarin is very intelligent," she retaliated. "And if you judge your precious quarry a place where angels fear to tread, I wonder you would think it sensible to plan a garden here, when you might better fill it in and prevent others from falling to their deaths!''

"That is much too long a sentence," he pointed out kindly. "I suppose I must now instruct you in proper speech."

"Pish-posh!" retorted Valentina, with an irritated toss of her curls.

He shook his head. "From bad to worse! However, I expect you are right, so let us go back."

"Go back? But we haven't even looked!"

"You just did. And you appear to think the dog fell to his death, if indeed he ventured in at all, so—"

"You are without doubt the most provoking man I ever met! Mandy! Here, boy! Man-dy!" There was no sign of movement. She said miserably, "Oh dear. What if the poor little creature is lying there, suffering?"

"Supposing, again," he scoffed, but then whistled shrilly. "Come on, Mandy. Come, old lad!"

Something warm and damp pushed into his hand. He whirled around. The mare was nuzzling him, watching him with her big soulful eyes. "Is your name Mandy, you obtuse clod?" he demanded, unobtrusively stroking the firm neck. "Go and devour some weeds."

Valentina was straining her eyes across the quarry, and she called again, her voice echoing through the great chasm. Distantly came a shriller sound, and seconds later a small shape could be seen springing vigorously over obstacles and around pools.

"He *is* down there!" exclaimed Valentina, overjoyed. "You see? You see?"

"Have a care, woman!" De Michel's arm swept about her waist and drew her back from the edge.

"Will he be able to climb out?" she asked, clinging to him as she peered anxiously at the small bounding form of the dog. De Michel did not reply. Glancing up at him, Valentina paused. He was watching her with a very odd expression. With small encouragement her imagination would have said there was a fondness in the dark eyes. Certainly, a smile such as she had never before witnessed hovered about his mouth. Wonderingly, she said, "Cousin Charles...? Let me go please. I am quite safe."

He did not let her go. What he did was pull her closer. His head bent lower. His eyes seemed to mesmerize her so that she forgot all about the perils of the Pekingese, and the quarry, and her anxious aunt. She was aware only of the lean face so close above her, the astonishing tenderness of his expression, the velvety softness of his eyes. She knew he was going to kiss her, and for an instant of madness, longed to yield up her lips.

Somewhere far away, Mandarin barked frenziedly.

Valentina jerked back her head. "What on earth are you doing?"

He smiled, and said, his breath soft on her cheek, "Don't be a peagoose. You know perfectly well." He leaned to her again, and she waged a desperate fight for sanity while every traitorous impulse yearned for his embrace.

"Let me go... at once!" she demanded feebly.

"Certainly not."

His lips touched hers. Briefly. Scaldingly. Shaken, she tore free and tried to sound properly affronted. "You are—are a positive rake, sir!"

"I admit I try to keep a positive attitude." He sighed. "Though it seems hard when one may not bestow a cousinly kiss on—"

"*Cousinly!* It did not impress me—"

"That is not kind," he interrupted, aggrieved. "I may not be a positive rake, but I've had few complaints."

"What you are is impossible! You had no right to do so bold a thing!"

"I had every right to expect encouragement. But was instead granted the merest pittance, so I go unconsoled to my doom." He moved to the steps.

Valentina gave a shocked cry and seized his arm. "You have wrenched your ankle! You cannot go down there!"

"Pray do not fly up into the boughs, Miss Umpire. That foolish animal cannot climb up. Ergo, I must climb down."

"But—it looks so horribly sheer! Is there no other way?"

He detached her clutching fingers and patted her cheek. "There was, of course. But the people who quarried this place overworked their path, and it collapsed. Lacking wings, this is the only way, until new grading is done."

Mandarin, who had made several abortive scrambles up the cliff face, now sat down, whining, and holding up one paw.

"Only look how the brute seeks to manipulate us," said de Michel. "He's afraid I might change my mind, so is adding pathos to the drama. Gad!"

Valentina gripped her hands together, and watched tensely. He trod confidently down those hazardous steps, but kept one hand on the rock wall. Glancing up at her, he paused.

She called in quick anxiety, "What is it? Does your foot pain you?"

"Terribly. And I cannot but wonder why I am going down for that foolish brute, when you are up there, looking so..."

"So...?" she prompted softly.

"So un-cousinly," he said, and with the flicker of a grin, took the next step.

Valentina smiled, then was holding her breath as he came to the end of the rebuilt steps. "Do be careful," she whispered. "Oh, *do* be careful!"

Again, the wind-blown dark head lifted. Interested, he enquired, "Are you praying for me?"

"No," she lied.

"Hmm. You looked as though you were. Pity."

A second later, Valentina was gasping out prayers in earnest, for having negotiated several of the crumbling steps successfully, the next one disintegrated beneath him, and in a shower of rocks and gravel, he was falling.

CHAPTER FIVE

VALENTINA WAS ON THE LAST of the reinforced steps when de Michel's roar halted her.

"Do not—*dare!*"

She gave a sob of relief. He was sitting up. "Thank God!" she gulped. "I thought you were killed. Are you badly hurt?"

"Probably. And you will definitely be hurt if you take one more step. Go back at once, madam!"

Moving cautiously, he got to his feet. She heard him swear and, reassured, clambered back to the top.

De Michel scrambled up the sheer slope, Mandarin securely tucked under one arm. Rocks and shale showered down with every step. When he slid back several feet, staggering to preserve his balance, Valentina closed her eyes, unable to watch. Peeping between her fingers after a short period during which there had been no sounds of a disaster, she saw that he had at last reached the first of the dependable steps. He was limping badly. Valentina edged as close as she dared, and reached out. He passed a cowed small dog to her. She put Mandarin down and reached out again. She had seldom been more relieved than when her cousin's scratched and dirty fingers closed around her own.

"Here," she said, supporting his faltering steps. "Lean on me."

He leaned on her until they reached the cart, then sat down abruptly, closing his eyes. His clothing was tattered and dusty, and the bloody graze on his chin was in stark contrast to the pale face. Frightened, Valentina knelt beside him. He looked at her, smiled feebly, and sagged. With a shocked cry she flung her arms around him steadying him. Mandarin trotted over and sniffed at his rescuer curiously.

"You naughty dog," scolded Valentina. "Only see what you've done!"

De Michel said with a sigh, "I have given up my life for you, stupid animal." His head drooped to Valentina's shoulder. "I think . . . my back is broke."

"Of course it isn't, or you would not have been able to climb up that dreadful cliff!"

"Oh. Then it must be my head. Doubtless my poor skull is crushed. I shall expire here, in your soft, warm arms." His head rolled, and one dark eye opened to peer up at her. "Would you kiss a dying man, Cousin Tina?"

"Yes. But I think you are not dying, and also that you are a considerable rascal, Cousin Charles."

He closed his eyes and moaned pathetically. Not a little anxious, Valentina knew that he was making light of his injuries so as not to alarm her, but both the knees were torn out of his buckskin breeches, revealing bloody abrasions, and the cut on his hand was bleeding again. She rested one fingertip on his cheek, and he lifted his head and blinked at her, smiling hopefully.

"Have you relented?"

Valentina bit her lip, then against all propriety swooped down to deposit a hurried peck on his cheek.

"Now that," he complained, "was a *very* cousinly kiss!"

"That was for bravery," she said.

His eyes began to gleam. "I think I must have a better one." His arm was suddenly about her again.

"No! Charles! Behave yourself!"

"How can you be so miserly? Consider my generosity. I allowed you to browbeat me into letting you live in my mansion—"

"Browbeat!"

"I rescued your silly sister from her own follies—"

"She is *not* silly!"

"I helped you maudle your sheet—"

"Mangle, foolish man."

"And in return you tried to strangle me. And it is unkind to laugh. I let you play, and you rewarded me by ruining my game of rounders, for Johnny was most definitely not 'out' as you claimed."

"His right foot was quite three inches outside the square! Charles, let me go!"

Ignoring her struggles, he continued to enumerate his grievances. "Each time I come near you or your family I am wounded! Only look at me now—a pitiful sight, and yet when I beg the slightest consolation—"

Something in their relationship had most definitely changed, thought Valentina. The shocking thing was that she found herself liking it. And to become too fond of this of all men, would be disastrous. "You have had your consolation," she said firmly. "I do not care to be mauled, sir!"

"Good, then we'll get it over quickly, which would be advisable, since I'll likely expire of my wounds at any instant." His head drooped again.

The arm about her slackened. Valentina peered at him. He really did look very bad. She said gently, "Please try to get up."

"I cannot," he sighed. "I'm weak as a cat and—" His body became rigid. He let out a sudden howl of rage that fairly terrified her, and forgetting his weakness sprang to his feet. "Wretched brute!" he roared.

Perhaps this was a brainstorm! Perhaps he really had broken his head! Dismayed, Valentina stood up and followed as he limped to the edge once more. "Whatever is it? Charles, pray do not go so close."

"Ingrate," he shouted, shaking his fist at the quarry floor.

Valentina looked down. Far below was Mandarin, in hot pursuit of a quail. "Oh dear!" she whispered.

"You may stay there till you starve, repellant creature!"

"Mandy!" called Valentina sternly. "Come back at once!"

Whether the Pekingese realized he had gone his length, or whether it suited him to show off, it would be difficult to say. He halted and looked back, then without the slightest difficulty scrambled up the precipitous path and came to join them, very dirty, but with his tongue lolling happily.

Not daring to look at de Michel, Valentina walked quickly to the cart and took up the reins. Mandarin at once leapt to the seat. Valentina said, "Can you manage, Charles?"

He folded his arms and ignoring her twitching mouth replied with regal dignity, "You may take your choice, madam. Either that revolting animal is ejected from the vehicle, or your victimized cousin will somehow contrive to walk all the way home."

Valentina told Mandarin sternly that he was a very bad dog and put him down.

De Michel clambered painfully to the seat and glared at the Pekingese who promptly sat down and whined, lifting one paw.

"Not this time, you Machiavellian Chinaman," growled de Michel. "Not this time!"

THE NEXT WEEK they made a concerted effort to complete the work de Michel had allotted them. The days seemed to fly past, and even Sidonie began to be apprehensive and to put in her fair share of work. Much to the ire of Horace, who was no cat lover, the mother cat began to invade the house. Mandarin also took a dim view of this, and the cat's future was in doubt until the day she caught a rat in the pantry. She was thereupon accepted as a member of the household, dubbed Mrs. Read (because she seemed to prefer the library) and became a fixture. Lady Rustwick was overjoyed by Mandarin's safe return, and sent Horace to the steward's cottage with a letter full of gratitude and admiration for "dear Charles" and his "courageous intrepidity" in having rescued the dog. Valentina, who had given her family a rather expurgated version of the incident, could picture de Michel's reaction and chuckled to herself. She did not see him during that week, but Lord Stane rode over every day and informed them that his host was quite recovered of his injuries and was working hard at the quarry. The young peer's blue eyes seldom left Sidonie's piquant features, a fact which Ashford found hilarious. He always teased his sister after these visits and while they were taking their luncheon on Saturday afternoon, asked how she would like to be Lady Stane.

"Much chance of that," Sidonie answered huffily. "What gentleman would offer for a penniless girl who exists only on her cousin's charity? I make no doubt Charles has told him all about us. About me, especially."

"Nonsense, child," said Lady Clara. "Your cousin is a gentleman and would not stoop to such vulgar behaviour."

Sidonie closed her lips, but after her aunt had left the table and gone to help Horace work in one of the second-floor bedrooms, she observed darkly that not everyone held such a good opinion of de Michel. "The whole County is talking. Mr. Roger Vokes says all the neighbours are very sure Charles is a Bonapartist, and it is but a matter of time before he is arrested."

Valentina turned alarmed eyes to her brother. "Arrest? Have you heard tell of this?"

Ashford, who had ridden into Leominster the previous day to exchange an armful of library books, shrugged his shoulders. "I did hear something of the sort, I'll not deny it, but I'd place no reliance on what young Vokes says. He's a rattle if ever I saw one, and can talk only of how his father means to buy him a pair of colours next year.'' He scowled darkly. ''Besides, de Michel knows what is being said of him. He should defend himself.''

''Joan Locks says he is forever skulking about at night,'' put in Sidonie. ''And that he is cruel to his poor mama, and will not let her go out in the local society, nor entertain, for fear she might say something she should not! Something that would cost him his head!''

Ashford said, ''I'd think you would realize that it is natural for Miss Locks to talk against de Michel. Lady Locks is her aunt, and ran off with him.''

Triumphant, Sidonie retorted, ''Which last certainly does not add to his character, save to blacken it.''

Valentina could only agree. She was quieter than usual that evening, and Ashford beat her twice at draughts. Aunt Clara said with some concern that dear Tina had been working much too hard, and urged her to retire early. Valentina followed her advice, but could not sleep, and lay awake for a long time, watching the warm night wind stir the bed curtains.

Her thoughts turned, as they often did, to the village green and their hilarious game of rounders. She had thoroughly enjoyed herself that day, probably because of the break in the monotony of scrubbing and cleaning and hard work. But even as the thought dawned, denial came with it. The fact was that she did not find her life here monotonous. Hard, certainly. But she loved the peace and beauty of the country, and the people she'd met had been so warm and friendly.

Further, she was beginning to enjoy restoring the old house; it was rather exciting to clean a dulled nondescript floor and watch a glory of beautifully inlaid woods come to life from under all the dirt; or to discover splendid carvings hidden by the thick smoke stain on a mantelpiece. Even Ashford had given a shout of excitement this morning when he'd washed an unusual octagonal window in one of the tower bedchambers and found under the heavy coating of dirt a most elegant design of stained glass. With the investment of some funds for paint, new furnishings, and the many repairs that Leslie and Horace could not accomplish, Wyenott Towers could be a lovely and gracious home.

She puzzled over the enigma that was their cousin. During the game of rounders in Wye Dilly, the harshly cynical Charles de Michel had vanished, and in his place had appeared a pleasant young man with a merry wit and a whimsical sense of humour. He had grumbled about the children, true, saying that they'd "badgered" him into playing their games. But even as he'd said it, his eyes had held that deep glint of laughter. Mrs. Bellewood had said, "...the children cannot keep away from him." More than that, they very obviously adored him, and despite his offhand air, Valentina suspected the feeling was mutual. He had spoken unkindly of the slothful mare, and later she'd seen his bronzed hand furtively caress the animal. And then there had been the business with Mandarin. A fiasco, at best, but the fact remained that even with a weakened ankle Charles had hesitated not one moment to venture down that horrid cliff and help the dog.

Why must he hide his kinder side? Was he afraid people would judge it a weakness that he liked children, and was fond of animals? She frowned. More to the point, why did she lie here, thinking of him? She must not allow one golden afternoon to blind her to the fact that there was another Charles de Michel. An unprincipled rake who would steal a loving husband's lady away from him and break his heart. A formidable duellist who had faced his victim at twelve paces and come near to killing him. A man of whom treason and treachery were whispered, who was unkind to his beautiful mother, and who rode out late at night with murder written in his face.

He had kissed her, and her heart had leapt. It still leapt whenever she dared recall that moment, but the truth was that it had been a dishonourable act on his part, and stupid weakness on hers. She turned restlessly onto her right side. Cousin Charles was a very bad man. When he chose, however, he could be too charming for one's peace of mind. How fortunate that she had been forewarned, so that she could dismiss him from her thoughts completely.

Having decided which, she fell asleep hearing him complain, "... a *very* cousinly kiss..."

ON SUNDAY MORNING a blustery wind hurried the clouds and whipped the treetops about. The long walk to Wye Dilly presented no deterrent to the three ladies of Wyenott Towers, but the thought of arriving at Church wind-blown and dishevelled was daunting.

They were delighted when a luxurious barouche drove to the front door, and Mr. Roger Vokes presented himself to ask if he might have the honour of conveying them to morning service. He was a rather toothy young gentleman of eighteen years, and quite obviously smitten by Sidonie. A generous allowance from his indulgent parent allowed him all the excesses of an aspiring dandy. His high shirt-points came near to obstructing his vision, his splendid shoulders were at startling variance with an overall skin-and-bone appearance, causing one to suspect a heavy use of padding, and the number of fobs and seals that decorated his thin waistline brought a twinkle to Lady Clara's shrewd eyes. His manners were nice however, and my lady accepted his offer gratefully.

It was a little crowded in the barouche, for Miss Harriet Vokes had accompanied her brother, and although only sixteen, she was as fat as he was lean. By the time Lady Clara, Sidonie, Valentina, and Mr. Vokes had joined her, skirts were crushed and bonnets in rather perilous proximity. Ashford, who had chosen to ride, glanced inside and grinned appreciatively, and Valentina envied him his male freedom from elaborate bonnets, and long skirts.

St. Peter and Paul's was situated at the western edge of Wye Dilly, and so quaint and tiny that Valentina thought it might have managed with but one saint to grace its name. It boasted a superb choir loft and although there were only six choirboys, they sang like angels. One of these glowingly spotless boys stared fixedly at Valentina, and she recognized him at last as Johnny, the grubby little bowler whom she had ousted from their rounders game because his foot had been outside the square. Amused by the resentment in his well-scrubbed little face, she concentrated on the sermon.

The vicar was a tall middle-aged gentleman with an amiable countenance and earnest brown eyes. He had taken "The Patience of Job" for his subject, and had he stuck to his notes might have preached a fine sermon. He tended to go off at tangents, however, with the result that his message became involved and confusing, and Valentina's was not the only attention that wandered. Her surreptitious glances around the sanctuary revealed no sign of de Michel. Lord Stane escorted Madame de Michel. Sir Derwent Locks was present. There were many military gentlemen in the congregation, several with ladies, one of whom wore a most fetching little bonnet of pale green straw with green feathers curling over the poke.

When the service ended, and they were shaking hands with the vicar, he presented this same damsel as his second daughter. Miss Abigail Tembury was very fair with pale clear skin and her father's big brown eyes. She was shy and soft of voice, her prettiness more that of unspoiled youth and gentleness than of fine bones or any real claim to beauty. Valentina moved on and looked about for Sidonie and Aunt Clara, both of whom had drifted away. When she turned back to Ashford, she was surprised to see him still beside Miss Tembury, an expression of rapt awe on his handsome face. 'Good gracious,' she thought. 'If ever there was a girl who will *not* do for my dashing brother!'

Her attention was diverted by the sight of Sidonie chatting animatedly with Sir Derwent Locks. Nearby, Aunt Clara was engaged in deep converse with the vicar's wife, a stout, fair-haired lady. 'That is just how Miss Tembury will look twenty years from now,' thought Valentina, and gave an inward chuckle at the thought of the volatile Ashford wed to so placid a creature. Her amusement faded as Sidonie's musical laugh rang out. Locks appeared entranced, as well he might, for Sidonie was a vision in a pale pink tunic with small gold buttons at the neck and hemline, worn over a white muslin dress trimmed with gold thread. Her bonnet was white, with pink velvet ribbons, and her reticule was of the same pink velvet, tied with gold braid. Many admiring glances came her way and young Vokes and Lord Stane joined the rapidly growing group of young men gathered about the little beauty. Despite the competition Locks was all amiability, but although Valentina pitied him, she could not quite like the man. His violent outburst at the Towers she judged to have been in poor taste and she did not doubt that the implacable hatred he had revealed, still dwelt just below that smile. She moved towards her sister, but turned aside when her name was uttered in a sweetly melodious voice.

Madame de Michel was beautiful, as ever. She had chosen a high-necked gown of pale green silk with an inset yoke of embroidered green lawn. Her elbow-length mittens were cream, and a small flowered silk hat was perched on her fair curls.

"Dearest child," said Madame, embracing her niece gracefully. "How exquisite you are in your twilled muslin. That particular shade of fawn makes your eyes look like great amber jewels!''

"Bless you, Aunt! Most people cast one glance at Sidonie and her spinster sister disappears.''

"What fustian! Your sister is adorable as a kitten, but—''

"Oh, no!'' interposed Valentina, laughing. "That must make me a cat!''

"Never judge it an opprobrious designation, my dear. It is an appellation often sent my way by other women, but,'' Madame chuckled, "I take it as a compliment, for is there anything more sleek, more gracefully mysterious and sensual than a well-cared-for cat?''

Valentina agreed laughingly, and they walked arm in arm to the lane. "Do you go home in your carriage, ma'am?'' she asked, glancing along the line of vehicles drawing up before the gates.

"Stane was so kind as to fetch me here,'' answered Madame. "But it is so pleasant now the wind has dropped, I think I shall walk home. I fancy you are driving. Which is your carriage?''

"I wish I might claim one. Alas, we lack such a luxury these days. Roger Vokes brought us, but to say truth it was rather a crush, and I mean to follow your example and walk back.''

"I suppose,'' said Madame rather wistfully, "you would not care to walk a little way with me? I have longed to talk to you, and I cannot say when I may be allowed—I mean, when I may come to the Towers again.''

A tiny frown creased Valentina's smooth brow, 'May be *allowed?*' she thought. 'Good heavens! Is the poor woman a prisoner?' She at once told her aunt she would be delighted to bear her company, and tipped an aimless-looking young boy to tell Lady Rustwick that Miss Ashford would walk home.

Madame was rather pathetically grateful for her niece's company, and they started off, several of the military gentlemen looking after them with marked interest.

The air was warmer now, and full of the scents of summer. The lane curved westward between tall hedgerows fringed with the bright faces of lupins, buttercups, and larkspur. The sky was a clear, dark blue against which the varying greens of shrubs and trees spread a verdant frieze. "How lovely it all is," said Valentina.

"You enjoy the country, don't you my dear?"

"Oh, I do. Not that I dislike Town. But—Herefordshire is so much more beautiful than I had expected. One thinks only of the Home Counties when one is a Londoner, you know, and— Oh, but what nonsense I do talk! You have been so much about the world. Certainly, you know the City better than I do."

"And miss it so," sighed Madame. "My dear, dear London. Sometimes, I—I think I will die of..." her voice broke, "of pure loneliness."

Horrified to see the lady turned slightly away, one hand pressed to her mouth in agitation, Valentina linked arms with her and exclaimed, "But dear Aunt, you have a splendid house in Town. Surely Charles would open it if he understood how miserable you are?''

''How I wish that were so, but my son does not like Town, alas.''

''That is his right, of course. But would you be uneasy to open the house without his company?''

''Good heavens, of course not! Do you take me for a green girl? I would like it of all things.'' The brief flash of excitement faded, and the shapely lips drooped once more. ''But he is quite adamant.''

Perhaps, thought Valentina, Charles did not want to worry his mama with the fact of his financial embarrassments. She said gently, ''I expect it is very costly to run so large a house.''

''Is that what he told you?'' Madame smiled with faint bitterness. ''I should not grumble. He can be very generous at times, and is devoted to me.''

''Save that he keeps you buried in the country when you long for Town.''

''True. I'd not mind it so much, if I could but see my friends. Just . . . now and then. When my beloved husband was alive—oh, the parties we had, dear niece!'' Her blue eyes began to sparkle and a little flush lit her cheeks as she remembered past joys. ''The long lines of carriages driving up to our door; the gowns and jewels, the merry chatter, the laughter! How terrible it is to be denied laughter! When he was well enough, Henri used to take me driving in the Park every afternoon. Always, there was some friend to greet. Even when his health began to fail, the dear man would insist I drive out. I never lacked for gallants to escort me to the theatre or the opera; to balls and routs and breakfasts! It was a world of joy—a world I never thought to leave. But—'' She shrugged; the animation went out of her face, and she said wryly, ''Ah well, I have had my happy years. Only look at you, poor darling. Young and lovely, working your pretty fingers to the bone, and condemned to this isolation when you should be breaking hearts and enjoying life.''

''But I do enjoy life, ma'am. No, truly, I am not much inclined for the social whirl. I'll own I miss my friends, but Sidonie is the one who longs for the London excitements. She shares your love for parties and—'' She broke off, a daring thought coming to mind. ''Aunt,'' she said slowly, ''suppose we were to give a party at the Towers?''

Madame gripped her hands with a little squeal of excitement. ''Oh! What a marvellous idea! Would you?''

''Yes indeed! We all would love it. I'm afraid it could not be a glittering affair, for our funds are small, but the dear old house looks much better already.''

''I will have it catered. Oh, if I could but send to Gunter's! But there is a quite respectable firm in Hereford! I shall write to them tonight! You and Sidonie must have new gowns, and you will need servants, but the caterers will see to that! Might I invite a few of my friends?''

Touched because of the radiance that now brightened her aunt's eyes, Valentina said, ''Of course! That is my whole thought. But, will Charles—''

''He must not know until it is too late for him to stop us,'' said Madame with a giggle. ''And since he'll not have had to pay a penny, he will be pleased. Oh, Valentina, what a delight you are! I will drive over on Wednesday afternoon, and you must have all the measurements and your patterns ready for me so I can order gowns for you and Sidonie. We will set the date, and— Ah, good afternoon, Major. How lovely to see you!'' She waved merrily to the mounted officer who walked his bay mare towards them, and lowering her voice added, ''Valentina, my love, will you excuse me? This is a dear friend, and doubtless wants to talk of old times. Until Wednesday, my dearest child. Truly, you cannot know how happy you have made me!''

VALENTINA STRAIGHTENED her sun bonnet and leaned back on her heels. ''It's hot work,'' she said breathlessly.

On his knees nearby, digging industriously, Ashford agreed, ''And only look at all the stuff we've pulled out. How Cousin Charles could have let it become so overgrown, is beyond me. Miss Tembury says it was the prettiest of estates once. Except for the quarry, of course. And the Vicar said in his young days there was a line of trees, screening off that area.''

''Well, they're gone now. What a pity. You know, Leslie, this old place could be quite lovely.'' She spoke a trifle hesitantly, fully expecting him to respond with some scornful remark comparing the overgrown jungle of a garden with the orderly delights of Hyde Park.

Surprising her, he said cheerfully, ''Very true. Drat you! Come up, you brute! Miss Tembury said they were elm trees and caught some nasty disease. Don't remember what.'' He heaved at a recalcitrant root.

"She is surprisingly knowledgeable. Who'd have expected such a dainty little morsel to have such an interest in horticulture?"

'Aha!' thought Valentina, and said, "Has she so? Perhaps the vicar is an enthusiast."

"Isn't he just! You should see—" Here, he gave a great tug, the root abandoned the struggle, and the young gentleman tumbled backwards.

A silvery peal of laughter greeted this small embarrassment. Sidonie ran from the house to dance around her prostrate brother, and, planting one little foot on his ribs, announced, "This dragon being duly slain, I claim the carcass, for England and St. George!"

"Do you, by Jove!" Ashford made a quick grab for her ankle and pulled, caught her as she fell, squealing, and sat with her on his lap, laughing at her. "How dare you name me dragon, when forsooth I am St. George?"

"Tush," she said irreverently, pinching the end of his nose and twisting from his hold. "We do not all look at you with the dazzled eyes of an Abigail Tembury, brother mine!"

"You little scamp," he said, reddening and glancing at Valentina from under his lashes.

"Has St. George told you where he goes when he rides out in the evenings, Tina?" Sidonie took up the clump of iris tubers and inspected them. "Or why he has of late become so interested in helping Cousin Charles at his horrid quarry?" She danced away as her victim made a lunge for her, and pausing just out of reach, tossed the roots onto Ashford's head and trilled, "Or for whom is a certain pretty bauble in the dragon's lair, which—'' She shrieked and sped into the house with Ashford racing in grim pursuit.

Left alone, Valentina pondered her brother's interest in Miss Tembury. The shy girl was a far cry from his London flirts, or the sprightly heiress who had been so mad for him in Sussex. Still, it was foolish to make a molehill into a mountain. Ashford was not yet twenty, and his future unsettled. It would be several years before he was ready to form a lasting attachment for any lady. Even so, Abigail Tembury could not fail to be a good influence. Valentina pursed her lips thoughtfully. Perhaps she should have a word with Ashford about the ''certain pretty bauble'' Sidonie had mentioned. Mrs. Tembury was a gentle lady but unless one mistook her she was a stickler for proper behaviour; it would not do for Leslie to be giving Abigail gifts.

CHAPTER SIX

DE MICHEL'S NERVES tightened as he climbed the quarry steps in response to the hail, and he wondered if, somewhere along the line, he had erred.

The colonel who awaited him was a well set-up man on the light side of fifty; tall and trim, with a pair of keen brown eyes and a fine head of thick hair of that nondescript shade that is neither brown nor blonde. Dismounting, he handed the reins to the trooper who accompanied him, and requested that the horse be walked. The trooper went off, and the colonel put out a hand. "You're Mr. Charles de Michel, I believe. I was told I'd find you out here."

De Michel lifted muddy hands. "Better not, Colonel. This is dirty work."

"And hot on such a muggy day, I'll wager. Herbert Card. Lieutenant Colonel. Conducting a little investigation for the Horse Guards."

"Egad, of what am I suspect?" asked de Michel easily. "Concealing a regiment of Boney's Cuirassiers in my quarry?"

The colonel smiled. "You'd have the deuce of a time getting 'em down there. Excuse my curiosity sir, but—whatever d'you mean to do with it?"

Very sure that this was a diversionary tactic and that the man had not the least interest in his plans for the quarry, de Michel derived a wicked enjoyment from launching into a long and involved explanation. Card surprised him by seeming genuinely interested, asked some intelligent questions, and eventually took out a small notebook and requested that a drawing be made of the final plan. De Michel strove painfully and at length produced a rather bewildering sketch. "I fear I have not an artistic bone in my body," he said looking ruefully at his much corrected effort.

"Perhaps not," murmured the colonel, replacing the notebook in his pocket. "But—er, you *are* of mixed blood I understand?"

De Michel caught his breath. So here it was at last. He stood a little straighter. "I believe half the inhabitants of the British Isles can trace a Norman somewhere among their ancestors." The colonel said nothing but looked at him steadily. De Michel shrugged. *"Oui, Monsieur le Colonel."* He gave a flourishing bow. "I am proud to say my father was French. To the guillotine with me!"

Card looked amused. "Well that confirms it, certainly. However, I'm not here to arrest you, sir. Merely to enquire if you've noticed anything untoward of late. Any hint of spies—espionage, and so forth."

"Gad—no! Out here amongst the turnips?"

The colonel began to wander along the edge of the quarry, de Michel keeping pace with him. "We had a very clever little covey of spies in London some time ago," said Card. "We were closing in on them, but they vanished. Thought we'd stopped 'em. But it chances we've been experimenting with a new type of musket. Be dashed efficient if we can perfect it. Some of the sketches turned up missing.''

"From Whitehall? That's a bit of a jaunt from Leominster, Colonel.''

"Isn't it, though? The sketches were found again very shortly, apparently having been simply misfiled. A week ago a very bright young subaltern came home from Spain on sick leave, and headed straight for his parents' house in Leominster. The Royal Mail had been held up the previous night by a rank rider known as The Galloping Gent, presumably because his speech is cultured. The coachman enlivened the journey for his passengers by stopping at the very place where he'd been robbed, and pointed out where the villain had stood. One of the passengers was a newspaper writer, and insisted he be allowed to get out and make a quick sketch of the spot. Luckily, our subaltern got out too. He found a scrap of paper containing part of a detailed drawing, and was shrewd enough to recognize it for the fragment of an official document. He brought it to us at once. Whitehall matched it with a sketch of the experimental musket. It was identical.'' He paused, watching de Michel's expressionless face. "You see the ramifications, sir.''

"You reason that the original sheets were copied and then neatly replaced. Ergo, someone else has the plans for the new weapon and probably means to sell them. And the highest bidder undoubtedly would be Bonaparte.''

"Not only that, Mr. de Michel. My C.O. finds it most intriguing that the sketch should have been found here. So far, as you said, from London Town."

Silence prevailed for a minute or two.

Card murmured, "You—er, have a house in Town, have you not, sir?"

"I am also believed to be a Bonapartist, Colonel." De Michel stopped walking and faced the officer squarely. "I have enemies. I am very sure I have been informed against, *n'est-ce pas?*"

The colonel did not answer but stared into the dark eyes that met his own so unwaveringly. 'A damned cool customer,' he thought, and said, "It would be a waste of my time to ask if the charges against you are true. I will merely point out, sir, that if you are innocent it would behoove you to keep very careful watch on your neighbours, and report any suspicious incident to us without delay. I shall give myself the pleasure of calling on you in a day or two. Meanwhile, Mr. de Michel, I'd suggest you make no attempt to leave the area." He saluted briskly. "Good day to you, sir."

Silent, de Michel watched him mount up, start off, then rein around.

"Forgot to tell you," said Colonel Card. "The scrap of paper had part of a message written on the back. Unhappily, the words were illegible, but in place of a signature, there was a symbol at the foot of the page—the outline of a crown broken in two. The same symbol used by the London spy ring. Interesting, eh?" With a flourish of his riding crop, he rode away.

'Damn! Damn! Damn!' muttered Charles de Michel.

LADY CLARA WAS GREETED with a cheer when she
carried a tray of cold lemonade to the three who toiled
in the jungle-like "flower-bed" along the front of the
house, and they abandoned their labours and joined
her on the shady steps.

"What good progress you are making," she said,
casting an approving eye over the weeded beds and the
pile of plants they had uprooted. "Perhaps you should
stop now. It is so warm this afternoon."

With rare dedication Sidonie said, "It must be
done, dear. We want this poor old ruin to look as well
as possible for Aunt Ruth's friends."

"Ruth de Michel is not the only one who sent out
invitations," said Lady Clara, firing up as she always
did when she spoke of her beautiful sister-in-law. "I
gave Ruth the names of some of my own friends,
miss!"

Ashford mopped a handkerchief across his perspir-
ing and dirty face. "And so did I. So did Tina, and
likely de Michel also."

Sidonie gave a disdainful snort. "His list will be a
short one! From what people say, he has not a friend
to his name save that silly great Lord Samuel Stane.
And even he will likely back away when—" She
caught her brother's eye and did not finish the sentence.

Valentina put down the iris tuber she had been sep-
arating, and turned quickly enough to see the tense
exchange of glances. "What do you mean? Sid? Has
Lord Stane told you something about our cousin?"

"Cousin! He's not really our cousin. Henri de Michel was not even distantly related to us, and Aunt Ruth was only Papa's half-sister."

Suddenly blazingly angry, Valentina said, "What an unkind thing to say! Of course Charles is our cousin! You should be ashamed to cherish so bitter a grudge only because he refused to fall under your spell as other men do!"

Sidonie jumped up, flushed and furious. "You always defend him, don't you Valentina? Why? I hope it is not because you have a tendre for him! If it is, then *you* are the one should change your loyalties! Why do you think he has left his precious quarry these past three days?" She gave an angry titter. "He is not gone to London to look at the Queen, dear sister! The Tower, more like!"

Valentina's breath was snatched away, and she felt cold and afraid.

"What you need, miss, is a spanking," said Lady Clara. "And Charles came back from Town yesterday, so your drama of him languishing in the Tower is faulted!"

"Sid," grumbled Ashford, vexed. "Did I not tell you to keep your tongue between your teeth? One does not make such accusations lightly, especially in time of war."

Valentina demanded, "Did you fill her head with such rubbish, Leslie?"

"If you must know, Sir Derwent Locks and I have had several enlightening conversations." Sidonie tossed her head back, her manner that of Jeanne d'Arc confronting her tribunal. "And I daresay he should know whereof he speaks."

"Locks hates Charles," said Valentina, her eyes flashing, "and would stop at nothing to take his revenge."

"Aye," agreed Lady Clara. "And I should like to know when you exchanged all these vicious confidences with Sir Derwent Locks, who is nigh old enough to have fathered you, Miss Prattlebox!"

"He may be a little older," said Sidonie defiantly. "But he is a perfect gentleman. Besides, everyone knows our precious cousin for what he is, a half-breed and a traitor!"

"Have done!" cried Lady Clara, starting up wrathfully.

In a rare exercise of his position as acting head of their house, Ashford thundered, "That will do, miss! Go to your room at once, and I do not want to see your face again today!"

Sidonie's defiance crumbled, and with a smothered sob she fled.

THE SUN WAS LOW in the sky and the afternoon was cooler when Valentina led FitzMoke to the quarry path and peered downward. De Michel was perched on an outcropping, a watering can and a box of plants beside him. He was not working at the moment, instead sitting very still, frowning into space as though wrestling a knotty problem. He had already set out several cuttings on either side of the steps, but when she let her eyes wander the vast expanse of the quarry, his ef-

forts seemed so hopelessly inadequate as to be ludi-
crous.

FitzMoke brayed a greeting, and de Michel's head
jerked up. The frown vanished, and Valentina felt
strangely warmed by the immediate white gleam of his
smile. "Good afternoon, sir. No, pray do not get up.
I see you are making a start on your transformation."

He stood and she held her breath as, disregarding
the abyss behind him, he sprang lightly onto the steps.
"I have put out cuttings in several other places," he
told her, taking a large handkerchief from his pocket
and wiping his face with it. "But it is not surprising
that my poor efforts are easily overlooked. At present, anyway."

She gazed around again and murmured, "Do you
really mean to try and make it into a garden? It will
take years, surely?"

"Oh, yes. But when it is done, I may—I hope I
may—have created something beautiful where now,
thanks to man's greed, there is only ugliness." The
words had been spoken in a softer, dreaming voice,
and were no sooner uttered than he looked embarrassed and flushed a little. "You must excuse my appearance, Miss Tina," he added gruffly. "I had not
expected the pleasure of your company."

He wore an open-throated shirt and a dusty old
coat. His leather breeches were old and mud-stained,
and a scarlet Belcher neckerchief stood in place of a
cravat. With his bronzed skin, the dark, tousled hair,
the informal clothing, he looked wild and powerful
and rather excitingly masculine. Valentina's heart gave
an odd lurch, then began to gallop. 'Good heavens!'

she thought. 'It is happening again! I ought not to have come here!' She fought to keep her voice calm. "I am persuaded you would look extreme foolish were you to wear formal dress while you labour. Should you not hire some men to work with you?"

"Yes. And will do so. I'm not to that stage as yet, however, for I must first have sturdy steps built, the walls graded, soil brought in, the bottom cleared and lawns laid down. I only set these plants in because the Vicar was so kind as to donate them."

"I have brought you some donations also. Or at least, FitzMoke has. We were clearing the flower-beds and I thought perhaps you could use these poor dispossessed items."

He went at once to look into the panniers strapped to the little donkey's back. "Gad, what a jumble! What are they all—do you know?"

Valentina viewed the mass of roots and bulbs uncertainly. "Some are tulips, I think. And those are iris, of course. And the little ones I believe may be snowdrops and crocus. I know there were some delphiniums and peony, but...which is which, I cannot recollect. Does it matter? Surely, you have so much to accomplish, anything will help?"

He chuckled. "It will indeed, and I thank you for bringing them. The thing is, you know, each has special needs. It would be no use to put gladiolus where they would be blown down by the wind, or iris where they have no room to spread. They would do better on the lower terraces, which are not ready yet, alas."

She looked disheartened, and he added quickly, "But the snowdrops and crocus would be just right for—for that spot over there, and I can put the rest out somewhere, temporarily."

"Now that's a good notion," said Valentina, brightening. "You need a sort of warehouse area for them."

"A growing field?"

"Just so." She looked across the littered floor of the quarry again. "My goodness, it is vast! So much to be done. How can you put lawns down there, Charles? It looks a proper bog. Especially at the far end."

"It is." He moved to stand beside her. "I shall probably have to bring in surveyors and have it drained before—"

"Or make it into a lake," Valentina interposed excitedly. "Oh, that would be lovely! A lake all over that end, and where the rock juts out, you could have weeping willows, or some such!"

"Jove, but that's a capital idea! And back from the banks, we will need trees and shrubs. Lord knows what kind, though. I've so much to learn about this business. The climate here is comparatively mild, and I'd thought it would be nice to import foreign trees. Something a little different. But—" he shrugged wryly. "Something a lot costly, alas."

"Yes, were you to have them shipped full grown." She knit her brows. "My dearest friend married a Naval officer and they travel much about the world. I could write and ask her to send seeds, perhaps."

"Jupiter! Why did I not think of that! I've friends stationed over half the globe. I know they all would be willing to send me whatever they found that looked interesting. What a splendid collaborator you are, cousin! As a reward, I shall give you an extension of time, so that you are not obliged to work so hard. Two extra weeks, m'dear!" He seized her by the arms and whirled her around, and before she could object a smacking kiss was deposited on the end of her nose.

"Oh!" she exclaimed indignantly. "How dare you, sir!"

"Gad! If I didn't forget you don't care for your family to embrace you. Poor girl, I expect you cannot help having so cold a nature."

"I am not at all cold-natured," she spluttered. "You are—"

"Yes, I recall that you were kind enough to hold me to be a positive—er, individual. Which being the case I positively must make amends. Tell you what, I shall take it back!"

He swooped even as he spoke. His lips found hers. Valentina had the distinct impression that she had been struck by lightning.

"Drat," said de Michel. "Missed. I'll try to do better."

"Indeed you will not!" Dazedly aware that she was blushing, she pulled away. She should box the ears of the impertinent rake. She should at least make an appearance of being outraged, but he was looking down at her, his lean face framed by the hazy blue skies, his dark eyes alight with laughter. For once he looked happy and carefree with no trace of the cynicism that usually marked him. Valentina experienced an odd presentiment that she would always remember this moment, and instead of chastising him as she ought, all she could manage was to tell him he was past praying for, and thank him for the extension of time.

TRUE TO HER WORD, Madame de Michel drove to Wyenott Towers on Wednesday afternoon, ostensibly to take tea with the family. Valentina and Sidonie had been eagerly awaiting her arrival, and the lady was welcomed with exuberance and ushered into the now immaculate withdrawing room. Their work schedule was less taxing thanks to de Michel's having granted them more time, and the day's tasks had been completed by four o'clock. Ashford had walked off somewhere, probably to the Vicarage, and Lady Clara had happily accepted an invitation to tea at the home of Lady Berrington, a rather erratic elderly widow who was a pillar of the local society.

Madame Ruth made polite enquiries as to the wellbeing of her sister-in-law and her nephew, but it was quite apparent that she scarcely listened to the replies, and at once launched into chatter about the party.

This, Madame had decided, was to be held on the following Thursday. "Now about your gowns," she said gaily. "I adore the ones you have chosen, girls. Really, I do. But I have brought patterns which I think might better suit the occasion. This style, made up in creamy blue sarsenet would be lovely for you, Valentina. Do you not agree?"

Valentina gave a gasp. "But—Aunt! That is surely more properly an evening gown. I had thought we were to have an afternoon tea party."

Madame's eyebrows lifted. "Goodness! Had you? Then I have got it quite wrong. I'd envisioned a small after-dinner gathering, with perhaps a table or two of cards, and light refreshments. You should wear sapphires, my love. I've a nice pair of sapphire ear-rings I will lend you." She turned pages swiftly. "And here is the gown I chose for you, Sidonie." That damsel peeped and gave a squeak of excitement. Pleased, Madame smiled, and said she had seen some pink satin at McAllister's Emporium in Hereford that should do nicely. "It has the touch of salmon that will become you beautifully, and with a simple strand of pearls, you will be quite unbearably lovely."

On she went, obviously in a glow of happiness. Her servants were even now delivering the invitations. The guests were to arrive at half past eight, since most people kept country hours and they would not want to be too late going home. She had made arrangements for the refreshments, and a couple of extra servants would arrive at six o'clock on Thursday afternoon bringing everything necessary. "I have invited some very eligible young officers," she said, putting an arm around each of the sisters, and scanning them fondly. "I adore the brave men who fight for our beloved land. Besides," she added with a twinkle, "it is past time you two lovely creatures were enjoying life!"

Valentina was still pondering her remarks two days later when Madame's carriage arrived at the door to convey Miss Ashford and her sister to Leominster. Madame Ruth was not to accompany them on this expedition having sent word that she did not want to arouse her son's curiosity "at this stage of the game."

Sidonie was agog with excitement and could talk of nothing but the party, the gowns that were now being created, and the "very eligible young officers." It would be a welcome relief to see other male faces besides "Lord Silly Stane and that callow youth, Roger Vokes." The young peer was still in the neighbourhood and called, drove by, or walked past Wyenott Towers at every conceivable opportunity. Valentina, who liked his shy, honest face, and pitied his devotion, at once came to his defence, but her remonstrances were only half-hearted, for her mind was on other issues. Most of these centred around a warm afternoon atop the quarry, and the disgraceful behaviour of a certain gentleman who was as headstrong as he was notorious.

They journeyed through lush fields, emerald green in the sunlight, where fat sheep grazed contentedly; through well-tended orchards and hop kilns, with here and there the half-timbering of a farmhouse or a fine manor whose red stone may perhaps have been quarried at Wyenott Towers.

When at length they rattled into the old town, Valentina was enchanted by the picturesquely narrow streets lined with quaint half-timbered and medieval buildings. "What a lovely old place," she exclaimed. "Oh, I do hope we shall have time to see Grange Court—they say it is one of the most beautiful timber-framed houses in all England!"

More single-minded, Sidonie said anxiously that she did not see very many fashionable shops. "I do hope we will be able to purchase what we need here."

Knowing her sister's recklessness when shopping, Valentina cautioned, "We do but need evening slippers to match our new gowns, Sid. And we shall have to be very careful, for our funds are small, I'm afraid."

Predictably, Sidonie launched into a lament about their poverty, and was still pouting when they had left the carriage and were making their way up the very narrow High Street. She became even more glum when they found a draper's shop which had no shoes at all, and were directed to a tiny establishment a short distance along the street. It did not look promising, but once inside they found an excellent selection of ladies' footware, including some charming evening slippers. Both sisters were able to be fitted, and left cuttings of their dress material so that the slippers could be dyed to match. The clerk, obviously dazzled by Valentina, took down the directions and promised faithfully that the slippers would be delivered to Wyenott Towers next afternoon, and the sisters went on their way much cheered.

Sidonie's giggles over the infatuation of the shy little clerk changed to delight when she discerned a friend approaching, but Valentina was irritated. She suspected that Sir Derwent Locks was attempting to fix his interest with her sister, and that Sidonie, far less sophisticated than she thought herself, was flattered by the attentions of an older gentleman. Sir Derwent was overjoyed, he said, to have met the lovely Ashford ladies. Valentina was coolly polite. Guessing that Sidonie had told Locks they were to come to Leominster today, she lost no time in informing him that they meant to return at once to the Towers.

Sidonie was disappointed and said she had thought they might at least take luncheon before going home. Sir Derwent was all eagerness to show them about the old town. They must honour him with their company at luncheon. He would take them to The Royal Oak Hotel; Miss Valentina could not refuse, for the hotel's minstrel gallery was famous, and she would want to see it for herself. Afterwards, he would escort them to the Priory Church; they had of course heard of it. It was positively ancient, the original donor having been Lady Godiva's husband, Earl Leofric. The present structure was of red stone "Perhaps obtained from the ugly hole that mars your cousin's land, Miss Valentina."

Sidonie pleaded, Sir Derwent begged, and Valentina was made to feel such a tyrant that at length she reluctantly accepted the gentleman's invitation. The hotel was charming and the food excellent. The host was proud of the minstrel gallery which could be recessed or pulled out from the wall as required. He was demonstrating this clever device when a groom came with a message for Sir Derwent, and the baronet went a little distance away to talk with the man. The groom hurried out, and Sir Derwent lost no time in convincing the ladies that if they left now, it would take but another few minutes to view the Priory Church. He was so insistent that although Valentina would have liked to view the famous structure, her patience ran out and she said firmly that she had other obligations that could no longer be delayed.

Sir Derwent looked downcast, but insisted upon escorting them back to the stable where they had left their carriage. He led them off along an even more narrow thoroughfare than the High Street, which was, he said, called Draper's Row, the high-gabled roofs all but meeting over the street. It was a fascinating place and Valentina was beginning to regret the fast pace Locks set, when she heard an outburst of shouts and hooting.

The baronet halted at once. "Now what excitement is in progress, I wonder?" He turned into a narrow alley and thence to a small square where a noisy crowd of people jostled and shouted, all staring in the one direction.

Valentina caught a glimpse of military scarlet, then Sidonie exclaimed, "Good heavens! Tina—it is Cousin Charles!"

De Michel, several books under one arm, stood on the flagway facing an army officer, who was inspecting what appeared to be identification papers. Four grinning troopers watched this encounter, and the onlookers pushed and shoved and offered various uncomplimentary suggestions as to what should be done.

A countryman in gaiters and a snowy smock jeered, "Put 'un on a boat and send 'un back to Parus, Captain!"

"Aye, and sink it in mid-Channel," shouted another, this sally drawing a shout of laughter.

Valentina thought numbly, 'Dear God! He is so alone!'

"Well, well," murmured Locks, and seizing Valentina's elbow as she started forward, added a sharp,

"Unwise, dear lady. There's trouble brewing. Best stay clear."

Frightened, Sidonie cried, "Tina, for goodness' sake do not go to him. Everyone will think we're traitors, too!"

"I have heard nothing to prove my cousin *is* a traitor," said Valentina angrily, and tried to pull free of Locks' tightening grip.

The army officer's voice was clear and pompous as the hubbub died down. "I trust you do not mean to leave the county, Mr. de Michel?"

"Unless you've a warrant to detain me," said de Michel, just as clearly, "I think you may take your trust to the devil, sir!"

The captain looked taken aback. The troopers grinned behind their hands. Annoyed by such aristocratic hauteur, the crowd surged forward.

"We don't want him in Herefordshire, Captain," shouted someone raucously.

"If you bean't about to take him," shouted another man, "maybe us folks will get rid of the dirty furriner!"

"On a rail!"

"Aye! Fetch some tar and feathers!"

Valentina saw a gloating satisfaction in Locks' face. She said, "That man who just shouted out is your groom, is he not, sir?"

He said innocently, "I did not see. Perhaps so."

"You know very well it is he! And trying to do my cousin a mischief!"

Her words were all but lost in the uproar, for the mood of the crowd was becoming ugly. The troopers drifted away, obviously having no intention of keeping order. Besieged, de Michel looked grim and unyielding, and his fist made short work of a bully who deliberately jostled him. His action further displeased the crowd and more people pushed in behind Locks and his ladies so that they were swept forward. Everyone seemed to be shouting at once, oaths rang out, brawny shoulders shoved, gowns were crushed, and gentlemen were trying to get their ladies clear of what bade fair to be a nasty business.

Above the din, Locks shouted, "How shameful that you must witness that rogue's imminent arrest!"

"More shameful that it was deliberately contrived," she flared, putting her arm around Sidonie even as she was gripped with terror for de Michel.

The shot was deafening. Shouts, curses and shrieks ran out, then ceased as a commanding voice cried ringingly, "That will jolly well do!"

Valentina wrenched around. De Michel's hat was gone, the books had been knocked from his hold, and he looked dishevelled, but stood with fists clenched, fronting the mob with proud defiance. Standing at his left side, Lord Stane coolly blew smoke from his pistol. To de Michel's right side the Reverend Mr. Tembury said, "Come now, friends. This isn't the British way, is it?"

"He ain't British," howled a voice from the section of the crowd in which Locks' groom had last appeared. "He's a bloody damned foreigner and a traitor!"

"If you've proof of that, whoever you are," shouted de Michel. "Come forward and confront me like a man, and stop hiding behind—"

A rock flew, and he reeled back, one hand clapped to his head.

Valentina's heart seemed to stop.

"Hey!" shouted someone angrily. "That ain't fair dealing, you coves!"

"Coward," roared Stane, one arm supporting his staggering friend.

There was much neck craning and shouts of, "Who did it?"

Stane invited, "Come on, you sneaking weasel! Aim at me—I'm a touch easier target!"

This awoke the British admiration for loyalty and pluck. Grins began to replace scowls, and some laughs were heard.

A wag said, "Better take orf yer hat, mate. Brighten things up a bit!"

Much laughter as Stane obliged and the sun turned his red head to a flame.

The captain reappeared. "Move along," he ordered sharply. All brisk military efficiency, the troopers went into action, and the crowd began to disperse, not without a few threatening shouts about "Frog lovers."

Her heart still thundering, Valentina saw de Michel's dark head turn in her direction. He looked dazed, but his eyes widened with recognition.

A hand was tugging at her arm. She saw scorn come into her cousin's pale face, and turned to find Sir Derwent leaning to her ear.

"Dear lady," he said, smiling fondly at her, "I think we should depart."

Annoyed, she wrenched free, but when she looked again, de Michel was walking away, Stane, the Vicar, and the captain accompanying him.

"I cannot tell you," said Locks, "how sorry I am that you had to see your kinsman's shame."

"Which is as well," snapped Valentina, "since the only shameful conduct I witnessed was not that of my cousin! Thank you very much for luncheon, sir. Good day to you. Come, Sidonie."

The flash in her eyes, the heightened colour in her cheeks dissuaded Sir Derwent, and he was wise enough to bow and say no more.

Stalking away, raging, it eventually dawned on Valentina that her wilful sister was very quiet. It had been a sordid and horrible scene. The poor girl could very well be in a state of shock.

Concerned, Valentina linked arms with her sister and surveyed her anxiously. "Are you all right, dearest?"

Her eyes glowing, Sidonie murmured, "Was he not magnificent? Such valour! Such loyalty to his friend! How could I ever have thought him silly? Do you know what, Tina? I hope Stane does come to our party!"

"BUT—BUT WHERE did it all come from?" gasped Valentina, gazing in astonishment from the fine Turkish carpet to the rich red and gold brocade of the draperies, the elegant settees and chairs, the exquisitely inlaid tables, gleaming silver candelabra, and the several paintings Horace was unpacking.

"The carter said it was all arranged by de Michel, for delivery to Wyenott Towers, Miss," said the ex-sailor, his dark eyes slanting uneasily to her. "Do you think as we should have waited to unpack it?"

"What a difference it makes! And is it not charming?" trilled Sidonie, flitting from one new piece to the next. "All of the finest quality, and chosen with such a good eye for colour and style."

"When your Cousin Charles does something, he does it properly," said Lady Clara, holding up a small painting of a dashing Royalist cavalier. "This will look nicely above the credenza, I believe. What do you say, Valentina?"

"I am amazed," she answered. "Sid and I drive to Leominster to shop, and when we come home it is as if a magician had waved his magic wand.

"Don't it look nice?" Ashford came into the room carrying a large box. "Makes the old place halfway livable, eh Sid?"

"Livable! It looks heavenly." Sidonie executed a neat pirouette. "We shall have a glorious party, if only Cousin Charles does not come and put the damper on everything!"

Valentina said curtly, "Since he provided all this, I would hardly suppose he means to do so!" Her eyes clouded as she recollected her last glimpse of de Michel. She must have added to his humiliation by having witnessed it while apparently on the arm of his enemy.

Sidonie shrugged and tossed herself onto the plump cushions of the rosewood and gold brocade settee, only to spring up at once, her big eyes full of dismay. "Good gracious! I had not considered, but wherever shall we put all the coaches?"

Ashford laughed. "You allow your imagination free rein, as ever! We entertain a few of Aunt Ruth's close personal friends from Town. Not a large gathering, silly chit."

"I'll warrant Aunt Ruth has *thousands* of close friends," argued Sidonie pertly.

CHAPTER SEVEN

"HE HAS NOT TAKEN his dinner at home these past six nights." Lady Rustwick's voice came, muffled, from the cupboard she was sweeping out in the east tower. "One might think him to have moved into the Vicarage, and I'll own I am surprised that the Reverend Mr. Tembury allows Abigail to stay up so late. It was past midnight before Ashford crept in last night."

"I rather doubt Abigail keeps my brother talking at such an hour," said Valentina, washing the mantelpiece over the hearth between the two bedrooms. "You know how Mr. Tembury is inclined to ramble, and certainly Leslie will not wish to offend him."

"I trust that is the way of it. The boy has been so sleepy these past few mornings I've scarce had a word out of him. I'd not thought it a serious attachment. Faith, but I hope it is not! Here we are, poor as church mice, and the Temburys little better!"

"Save that they at least have the church," put in Valentina with a twinkle.

"And conversely, here is Sidonie sending Stane off with a flea in his ear," my lady went on. "And him a baron and full of juice."

Valentina clicked her tongue. "A fine example you set us with your use of English, Madam Aunt!"

"Oh, I know I'm a wicked old woman and use cant and make you ashamed of me," said her ladyship, and was at once rushed to, hugged and kissed, and told she was dearly loved and irreplaceable, and not to be such a widgeon.

"We are blessed," Valentina went on fondly, "with one aunt who is warm and kind and loving—if a little naughty at times; and another who is the epitome of style and sophistication, as well as being most generous."

"Pshaw!" snorted Lady Clara. "Hold the dustpan for me, child. I've no mind to bend so far. Ruth de Michel is generous as any bowing contractor or whatever is the name of those horrid fat snakes in the jungles. I've yet to see her do anything but what pleased herself!"

Valentina picked up the dustpan. "This party may make her happy, but has also made Sidonie happier than I've seen her in months. I cannot fault Aunt Ruth for that. There is little doubt but that Charles adores her. And when she speaks of Uncle Henri there comes such a look of sorrow into her eyes. I think she must have been a most devoted wife."

"Of a devotion most smothering," said Lady Clara with a grim nod. "A bowing contractor! Did I not say it?"

Valentina stared at her, but before she could speak,

"We've company coming, m'lady," bellowed Horace from the lower landing.

Valentina snatched off her cobwebby mob-cap. "Oh! Perhaps Aunt Ruth has brought the gowns!" She ran lightly to the stairs, then turned back, one hand on the rail. "And cheer up, dearest. Sidonie has changed her mind about Stane, and decided he is a knight in shining armour after all."

"Has she, by Jupiter," said my lady, brightening. "Perhaps the girl has a glimmer of wit hiding under all that hair!"

When Valentina rather breathlessly reached the ground floor, she fully expected to hear her sister greeting Madame de Michel. There was no sign of Sidonie, however, and the lady who was being handed up the steps by a bewigged and liveried footman was small and heavily veiled.

Valentina fled to the drawing room, and hid her apron behind a cushion on the elegant new settee.

Horace came in carrying a calling card on the silver salver but instead of proffering it to Valentina, whispered, "It's Lady Derwent Locks, Miss Tina. Shall I say you're not at home?"

Shocked and suddenly very nervous, Valentina said, "Heavens, no. I'm sure she saw me just now. Please show her in."

Lady Locks had put back her veil, and Valentina advanced to greet a pale-faced girl of about her own age, with glossy dark curls and great sad brown eyes.

"I know I have surprised you by calling, Miss Ashford," said her ladyship, refusing an offer of tea, but sitting beside Valentina. "It was good of you to receive me. Very few people will nowadays."

Valentina forced a smile. "We are not overburdened with callers, ma'am. Everyone knows we are penniless, and dwell here only by my cousin's charity."

"It is because of Charles that I have come to see you." Jennifer Locks' mittened hands were gripped tightly. Staring down at them, she said, "I can stay but a very few minutes. If my—my husband should find me..." She tightened her lips, then looked at Valentina searchingly. "I am quite ruined, you know. None of my lifelong friends will speak to me in public, though many have commiserated with me in private. Poor Charles is shunned and disgraced. And everybody believes the ugliness my husband set about in an attempt to cover up his own misdeeds."

She paused, looking so grieved that Valentina inserted gently, "You must not wish to speak of such personal matters, Lady Locks, and—"

"Please call me Jennifer," the dark girl interrupted. "And I beg you will hear me out. Charles comes occasionally to see me at my parents' home, when he is in Town. Something he said the other day, or perhaps it was the way he said it, convinced me that I must come and tell you the truth of things. It is a sad and perhaps all too familiar story. A great and true love, but a lack of either title or expectations; a most gallant young gentleman going out to India in a desperate attempt to make his fortune, only to—to die in a great cholera epidemic a year later." Her voice broke and she seemed overcome.

Touched, Valentina took one of the small restless hands and held it strongly. "This is painful for you, dear ma'am, and is not at all necessary. I do not hold my cousin in contempt because of all the rumours, if that is what you think." She was mildly surprised to realize this was true, and wondered why it should be so.

"Do you not?" cried Lady Locks eagerly. "Oh, I am so glad! But still, I want you to know the whole story. From the time of my come-out Sir Derwent was assiduous in his attentions. I was only seventeen, and he frightened me. I did not at all like him, and I was still hoping then, that my beloved Percy would come home and claim me." She gave a wan little smile. "After we received word of Percy's death, nothing seemed to matter anymore. I was quite ill for almost a year. When I recovered, Sir Derwent took up his courtship again. He was attentive, charming, incredibly generous. I felt almost guilty when I accepted him."

She paused again, then said earnestly, "I did not deceive him, Miss Ashford. I explained as kindly as I could how matters stood with me, but he laughed and said I was just a foolish little girl, and that he would make me love him. Only..." She sighed. "He did not. I discovered very soon that I had married a brutal man with a violent temper. I had insulted him, it would appear, when I at first rejected his advances, and further when I kept him waiting for so long before I accepted his offer. After I became his wife, his manner to me changed completely." Her eyes fell. She said in a low, halting voice, "He was—cruel...and took delight in—in humiliating me, even before the servants. When I was unable to provide him with an heir, he began to abuse me with his fists, as well as his words."

"My heavens!" exclaimed Valentina, horrified. "Why did you not return to your family?"

"I tried to. My husband caught me packing. He beat me, and said he knew I had taken a lover, and that he would kill Charles if I attempted to run away." The sad little smile flickered again. "It was all false. My love, Percy, had been Charles' dearest friend. Charles knew enough of Derwent Locks to beg me not to marry him. If only I had listened to him..." She shook her head regretfully. "But—that is neither here nor there. I did see Charles whenever I could, and it was because Derwent noticed I was always happier after our meetings that he built up his fantasy that Charles was my lover. Things went from bad to worse. One night Derwent was so...so bestial toward me that my maid was terrified. She rode to Charles' cottage and told him I was being murdered." Another pause. She said sombrely, "She was very likely right. Charles came at the gallop. He burst into the house. I need not tell you that there was a most dreadful fight. Charles beat Derwent soundly, then wiped his boots on him. All our servants watched, and they cheered when Derwent was vanquished."

Aghast, Valentina said, "And then Charles ran away with you?"

The dark head nodded. "All the way to my father's house where I have stayed ever since. My family were appalled when they saw me and heard what Charles had to say. My brother wanted to call Derwent out. Charles knew he would be killed, for my husband is an excellent shot, so Charles said he had the prior claim."

"Yes. I heard they fought. And that Charles won."

"Thank God he did. He went to see Derwent while he was recovering, and warned him that if he ever again attempted to hurt any member of my family, Charles would come back and finish what he'd started. I believe Derwent is very afraid of Charles now. He goes about uttering fearsome threats and telling the most horrid lies about us. He has worked incredible mischief by enlarging the rumours about Charles being a traitor, and he pays his men to do everything possible to blacken Charles' reputation, and to stir up public opinion against him. Your cousin has paid a high price for his gallantry."

Valentina was finding it difficult to conceal a soaring jubilation. She said, "I think I saw some of your husband's mischief-making a few days ago in Leominster. What a dreadful time you have had, ma'am. I am so sorry."

A small hand was placed on her sleeve. My lady said wistfully, "Thank you. Do you think—perhaps—we might be friends?"

Valentina smiled. "It would be my honour. But, if we arc to be friends, I feel emboldened to ask a question. Whatever shall you do? You are still so young and lovely. Shall you seek a Bill of Divorcement? You would have ample grounds, I should think."

"I might, if only Charles were not under such a cloud. As it is—well, people like to believe the worst, you know. My husband swears that Charles and I stole the Locks diamonds. They are truly magnificent. An exquisite necklace, earrings, a bracelet, and a ring. One might think people would realize that if Charles *was* my lover and we had such a prize, we could have fled the country long since. But—I swear to you, Miss Ashford, I never stole so much as a teaspoon from Sir Derwent Locks. No more did Charles!''

MADAME DE MICHEL'S carriage drove up after luncheon the following afternoon and Madame swept into the house followed by her dressmaker, a maid, and a footman who carried large boxes in which were the completed gowns. What excitement prevailed then! How Sidonie danced and clapped her little hands and squeaked with joy when the rich pink satin was lovingly unwrapped. How Valentina's hazel eyes sparkled with delight on beholding the shimmering enchantment of the creamy blue sarsenet, the delicate seed-pearls that edged the *décolleté* neckline and front closure, the long white silk evening gloves. Upstairs trooped the two girls, the footman, maid and dressmaker.

Lady Clara disliked being indebted to a woman she thoroughly detested, but to see her loved ones happy awoke in her a passion of gratitude. Madame was thanked repeatedly, Ashford was called in from his labours and added his own thanks until Madame cried out for mercy. Horace hurried away to prepare tea, and Madame sent her footman out to the coach to fetch in her sketchbook and crayons so that she might capture "the family beauties" in their finery.

Standing patiently, while pins and needles were busily employed, Valentina peeped at herself in the mirror. She had forgotten what a vast difference nice clothes could make, and was amazed by her transformation from a rather shabby young woman to a glowingly elegant creature being readied for a fashionable party.

"Now, we must brush out your hair, miss," said the maid, "and put on the necklace, for Madame wishes you to model the gown for her."

The dressmaker went hurrying to Sidonie's room to see how she was progressing, and Valentina submitted meekly while her hair was dressed and the sapphires fastened.

"Oooh!" exclaimed the maid, gazing at the finished product.

Fifteen minutes later, Ashford, who had been grumbling about the inordinate length of time it takes a female to try on a frock, sprang to his feet as Sidonie and Valentina came into the drawing room, hand in hand. "Bravo!" he cried, applauding heartily.

Lady Clara surged up from her chair, embraced her nieces tearfully, and said it was "such a joy" to see them looking elegant once more.

"What a lovely sight," exclaimed Madame, turning from Valentina, slender and graceful in the pale blue-green sarsenet, to Sidonie, like a dewy blushing little rose in the pink satin.

Sidonie cried ecstatically, "Oh, but I feel alive again!"

"Truly, we are most grateful, dear Aunt," said Valentina. "That Charles should have sent all this beautiful furniture; that you should be so good as to allow us this party, and now—"

"Enough! Enough! I implore you," cried Madame laughingly. "I can sustain no more gratitude. No—do not come and kiss me now. Rather, stand there by the hearth, the light will be perfect.'' Busied with crayons and sketchbook, she went on, "A step closer to your sister, Sidonie, so that you are just slightly in front of her. Perfect! This will not take long.''

Her hands flew in swift, sure strokes. Curious, Ashford stood and wandered to where he might peer over her shoulder. His eyebrows rose. "Jove, ma'am, you've the gift for it. I never drew a cat yet but what it looked like a stunted cow!''

Horace interrupted their laughter. "Colonel Card, my lady."

Ashford turned to the door in surprise. For some reason, Valentina experienced a stab of fear. Sidonie stared, and Madame Ruth paused, crayon in hand, glancing over her shoulder at the new arrival.

The tall army officer came briskly into the room, shook hands with Ashford, crossed to bow over my lady's hand, and clicked his heels, Germanic fashion, to Miss Ashford and Sidonie Ashford. 'Dashed pretty girls,' he thought appreciatively.

"And my sister-in-law, Madame Henri de Michel," said Lady Clara.

Madame turned to face him and the colonel received a full broadside from a pair of limpid cornflower-blue eyes. With a slow and provocative smile, she extended one dainty hand, looking up at this attractive man from under her long curling lashes.

For a moment Colonel Herbert Card did not move a muscle. Then he went to take that outstretched hand and hold it gingerly. "Your servant, ma'am."

"I think we have not met," murmured Madame. "Had you come to see Lady Rustwick?"

"To say truth, I had hoped to speak with Mr. Charles de Michel. Is he from home?"

"But no, for we no longer live here. My son and I occupy what was once the steward's cottage, some half-mile away." With an arch glance, she added, "If you can wait while I finish my sketch, you may accompany me home."

"Meanwhile," said Lady Clara, "you must take tea with us, Colonel."

"It will be my very great pleasure," said Card, occupying the chair she indicated.

"Are you to be stationed in the vicinity, sir?" asked Ashford.

"Only temporarily. I'm on a small investigation for the Horse Guards. As a matter of fact," his eyes turned again to Madame, "I had a chat with your son just recently, ma'am. Perhaps he mentioned it to you."

For the barest instant, Madame's smile was rather fixed, and her hand paused over her sketchbook. Then her crayon moved on smoothly. "No," she said, "he did not."

THE AIR WAS WARM that afternoon, and after Colonel Card had left, de Michel wandered onto the rear terrace of the old cottage. The lawns were bathed in a golden glow, the shadows of the trees lying black against the lush turf. From the flower-beds below the terrace came the scent of roses and the hum of bees. All was peaceful and charming, and so typically gentle and English. De Michel's mouth twisted and he gave a cynical grunt. Taking out his case of cigarillos, he lit one and sent smoke spiralling into the still air, and thought, 'What in the devil am I to do? And how much time have I?'

"Must you foul the air with your horrid smoke, Charles?"

He dropped the cigarillo at once and crushed it under his boot. "Your pardon, *Maman*. I thought you had gone upstairs to change." He turned, looking at her gravely, and knew she was angry. "You have made another conquest, I think."

His mother came and stood beside him, her lovely face studiedly expressionless. "And I am very sure you disapprove. As always."

"Of course."

Resentment flashed in her eyes. "You handled it crudely. I wonder you did not arouse his suspicion." He said nothing, and she went on, "Or is it already aroused? Why did you not tell me he had sought you out?"

He answered obliquely, "I've kept my eye on him."

"Oh, you've no need to tell me that." He did not respond, and his impassivity seemed to inflame her. She said on a note of desperation, "Charles, Charles—I cannot *endure* living like this! I *beg* of you, let me go back to Town. Or to Brighton. Away from this *dullness!*"

"I wish I could, ma'am, but you have left me no choice."

She whirled about with a muffled sob. "How can you be so disloyal?"

"That is all in the point of view, ma'am." And then, placing one hand gently on her bowed shoulder, he said, "My dear, I do what I must."

She flung around to face him again. "And despite the extreme danger you will likely bring down upon me, as well as yourself! You could not be so cruel if you cared for me."

"You know I always have loved you very—"

"Words! Empty words! My wishes, my safety mean nothing to you! Well, be warned—I will not permit this to go on!"

He said wistfully, "A threat, *Maman?* Have we come to this, then?"

Tall and lovely, she stood there, her dimpled chin high, her haughty gaze locked with his rueful one.

Sighing, he said, "I cannot change what I am, *ma chèrie.*"

"Do not dare call me that while you deliberately place my life in jeopardy! That sort of rubbishing nonsense I can do without!"

His head bowed, but he said nothing.

Watching the thick tumbled dark hair, her eyes softened. Her slim white hand went out to lift his chin. She murmured, "Ah—only see how sad you are! Do you remember when you were a little boy, how I would calm you when you were hurt or troubled?" Her fingers stroked his cheek. She sang in a low sweet voice,

Diamond tears? Ah, never weep dear,
All your fears I'll swiftly banish.
Hold my hand and I shall stay near
Till with dawn your troubles vanish.

"You always were there when most I needed you, *chère Maman*." He seized her hand and kissed it. "Did you think I had forgot?"

"Then, I beg of you—stop all these heroics! Your cause is lost. For both our sakes, stop—before it is too late."

A moment of silence, then he straightened his shoulders. "I cannot."

Her expression changed. With an inarticulate cry, she drove her hand so hard across his cheek that he was staggered. "Traitor!" she cried shrilly. "Ungrateful, unfeeling, worthless—traitor!"

And with a sob she ran back into the house and left him standing there motionless, staring blankly into the golden sunlit garden.

THE EXTRA SERVANTS arrived at two o'clock on the day of the party. As Madame Ruth had promised, they brought everything with them, including the sketch Madame had made of the Ashford sisters, now beautifully painted. This was much admired, and propped on the drawing-room mantelpiece where the guests would be able to see it.

Valentina was startled to find that she had not comprehended Madame's notion of "everything." The ranks of the "extra servants" had swollen a little; instead of two, there were six. The "everything" occupied four large waggons, two carts, four coaches, and a flock of "helpers" from the Hereford caterers. Speechless with astonishment, Valentina watched a parade of men carrying tubs, crates, boxes, and cases up the back steps and into the kitchen. An impressive

major-domo deigned Horace a glance that held in it
shock, disbelief, and contempt; then, with a thin
smile, forgot him.

The major-domo inspected the drawing room and
shuddered. The dining room caused him to roll his
eyes towards the ceiling. His exposure to the kitchen
evoked a yelp and the clutch of one shaking hand at
his aesthetic brow. He had not recovered from those
shocks when he suffered a larger one. Ashford erupted
into the kitchen wearing knee breeches so tight he
could scarcely walk and that terminated about an inch
above the knee. In the middle of an impassioned demand to know what "you fiendish females have done
to my garments", he became aware that several astonished strangers viewed his embarrassments. With
a very red face and a moan of mortification, he fled.
The major-domo began to suspect that this would be
a night to remember, and cheered up considerably.

The light repast Horace had intended to serve at five
o'clock never materialized. Instead, Lady Clara, Valentina, Sidonie and a still-shaken Ashford were served
a delightful meal in the breakfast parlour, waited upon
by silent-footed urbane menservants who anticipated
every need and performed their duties as though the
misplacement of a glass, an incorrectly folded nap-
kin, the rattle of serving spoon against bowl were
grounds for execution.

The sun was low in the sky when Madame's carriage drove up. She alighted, a vision in an extremely
décolleté cream taffeta gown, with an overdress of
dusty green lace. Her fair hair was dressed high on her
head, and she ran to the nearest mirror and inspected

herself anxiously, patting her curls and straightening
the beautifully carven jade necklace she wore. "How
exquisite you look, dearest," she said, cutting short
Valentina's thanks for the portrait. "My sapphires are
just right with that gown. I knew they would be." She
viewed her jade necklace dubiously. "If I but had my
emerald again..." She sighed, "How gauche you must
think me. Truly I do not begrudge it in the slightest.
Your dear papa meant only the best, and if his scheme
had worked, we all should have become rich. Besides,
if one gambles, one must accept the whims of Fate
without whining, no?"

Conscious of a pronounced sinking feeling, Valentina asked, "Do you refer to the Gatesford emerald,
aunt? The pendant bequeathed to you by your papa?"

"Yes. I do not remember my father, of course, for
I was but a babe when he died and Mama married
Clement Ashford. I was not allowed to wear my pendant until I married, if you please! And oh, but it was
so beautiful!"

"Do you say you loaned it to my father, ma'am?"

"John and I were always borrowing, back and
forth, for we were both wildly irresponsible, I fear.
Two scatterwits, my beloved Henri used to say. We
never kept accounts, but I fancy the emerald more
than balanced whatever I had owed your papa in the
past."

"M-more than *balanced?*" Valentina's voice
squeaked a little. She stammered. "But—but, Aunt—
it was worth a—a fortune!"

"John needed a fortune, dear. To invest in that
funny little German man's scheme for light or heat, or

some such thing, though Henri claimed most of the
cash went over the gaming tables. But never mind all
that. There you are, Ashford! Goodness, how handsome you are in evening dress! We'll have the carriages arriving soon, and you must form the reception
line. Tina, dearest, could you run up and hurry your
poor old Aunt along, do you think?'' She turned to
the major-domo and lapsed into French. "My dear
Jean-Paul, how very nice that you were able to handle things for me at such short notice. Now—as to the
accommodations for the horses, have you made sure
that..."

Valentina made her way up the stairs. She called
Lady Clara and Sidonie as one in a dream, noting
vaguely that her sister looked like a fairy princess, and
that Aunt Clara was majestic in purple satin and
pearls. All she could think of was the Gatesford emerald. Once, when she was quite small, she had seen
Madame Ruth wear the pendant, and could remember that even at that tender age she had been awed by
its size and beauty. That it had been of far greater
worth than any sum Papa had owed to Henri de Michel was beyond doubt. And Aunt Ruth had *given* it
to Papa! Stunned, she thought, 'We are here under
false pretences! Little wonder Charles was so disgusted when I tried to shame him into letting us stay!
He must *know* the balance of debt is on our side—not
his! And I told him we were part-owners of Wyenott
Towers!' She moaned faintly.

Two hours later, feeling that she was lost in a bad
dream, she paused on the threshold of the drawing
room wondering where on earth all these people had

come from. Each time a carriage had rolled up to the door she'd been sure it must be the last, but by nine o'clock guests were still arriving, and by ten she seemed to have shaken hands with half the army officers still in England. The conversation level had risen louder and louder. A trio of musicians who had appeared in the deeply recessed bay as if by magic were playing with optimistic verve, and small chance of being heard.

A hand slipped around Valentina's waist. Both Lady Clara and Sidonie had long since abandoned the reception line, and Ashford said with a broad grin, "I think we can go in now, don't you? Did ever you see such a crush? Aunt Ruth is in alt. And only look at Sid."

At the centre of a group of admirers, Sidonie held a glass of punch in one hand and her fan in the other, and fairly radiated happiness. Ruth de Michel drifted from one group to the next, exchanging greetings, exclaiming over this gown or that coiffure, as gracious as she was beautiful. The tall colonel who had visited them two days ago was present, very dashing in his dress uniform, and Ashford whispered in Valentina's ear, "See how Card watches Aunt Ruth. He's properly moonstruck, poor clod."

A liveried footman came up with a tray of glasses, and Ashford appropriated one for himself and one for Valentina. "Yes, it's champagne, love. But if your feet are as tired as mine, you've earned it. Drink up quickly, before anyone notices your depravity."

Valentina had seldom tasted champagne, and it seemed excessively potent. Only two sips made her head feel dizzy, and as soon as her brother left her, she set it aside. Lady Clara was chatting with the Vicar and his wife. Valentina wondered guiltily if her sampling of the champagne had brought the grim expression to her aunt's face. She barely had time for the thought however, before her own release from the reception line was noted and she was surrounded by an eager group of gentlemen.

At half past eleven, she managed to slip alone into the garden. A brisk wind had come up, and she wandered idly, grateful for the darkness and the cooler outside air. It was most rude, she knew, but she was hot and tired and had the headache, which seemed horridly unfair. After all these months of poverty she was at last wearing a really pretty new gown and attending the kind of jolly gathering she had missed more than she'd realized. She should be happy as a lark—or as Sidonie. Instead, she was utterly miserable. The Gatesford emerald haunted her. If Charles had been here, perhaps she could have relieved her conscience by explaining matters. Aunt Ruth had said that once he had discovered he was not expected to pay the cost he would be pleased to attend. But he had not come. Did he resent the fact that they'd kept the party a secret for so long? Or had his disgust of her deepened when he'd seen her with Derwent Locks at the Leominster fiasco?

Deep in thought, she wandered along the drive path. The sound of hooves brought her head up, and she saw a rider coming towards her.

A deep voice called, "It's only your tyrannical landlord."

"Oh," said Valentina, her heart giving a silly little jump.

He was closer now, and looking down at her bathed in the light of the three-quarter moon, said frowningly, "You're much too lovely a sight to be out here alone, Mistress Umpire! You Ashford women have a disturbing tendency to roam. Does lunacy run in your family perhaps?"

"I had not suspected it," she replied sweetly, giving him look for look. "Until very recently, that is," she added.

He grinned. "*Touché!* Dashed if I didn't forget I am part of your family, however distantly! Well, and I am hoist by my own petard!" He bowed with a flourish. "You won that suit, dear coz. Still, I insist upon knowing why and whither you wander. Are you perhaps off to work in my quarry?"

Watching his swinging dismount, she thought that he moved like a cat, lithe and smooth, with a ripple of powerful muscles. "Of course," she said, wiping the foolish smile from her face as he turned and began to walk along beside her. "Only I forgot to bring my spade."

"'Ware little Tina! I might have one tucked away in my saddlebags."

His horse did carry saddlebags. Eyeing them, she asked, "Do you leave us, Charles?"

He drew her to a halt. "Would it grieve you if I did?"

It came to her suddenly that it would grieve her very much. "Yes."

He was very close, looking down at her with an intensity that made her heart turn over, then start that dreadful tattoo again. "Tina..." His voice was low and husky.

"Because there is something I must say to you," she went on hurriedly. "When I first came here with my—my proposal, I did not know about—"

"I stand in an enchanted garden, under a summer moon, with a beautiful girl beside me," he interrupted, pulling her firmly into his arms. "And she wants to talk about proposals! You are fast, that's what it is, Miss Valentina Ashford...."

"*I* am!" she objected, more or less struggling.

He chuckled, and his lips brushed the end of her nose, making her quiver from head to toe.

She gasped, "No, Charles. I am trying to say—"

"Then I beg you will desist. You certainly did not come wandering out here with chitchat in mind." His eyes were smiling into hers with incredible tenderness. One long finger began to trace a path down her cheek, but checked abruptly, "Why *are* you wandering out here? And so exquisitely gowned! Do I obstruct a romantic assignation, perhaps?"

His voice was sharper, his eyes narrowed and suspicious.

"Had you supposed that I have no admirers?" she said archly.

How swift the return of the stormy look. "No. But if you are so ill-bred as to wander out after dark, to meet some lovesick ploughboy, I'll—"

"Spank me, and stretch him at your feet with a pistol ball in his head, I suppose!" Irked, she pulled away. "And what makes you think my suitor is 'some lovesick ploughboy?' I collect you judge me incapable of attracting a—a nobleman!"

"An ignoble nobleman who would skulk out at night to flirt with a lady of Quality, with no thought to her reputation or his honour! Besides, the only nobleman I've seen lurking about Wyenott Towers of late is so bewitched by your pretty little brat of a sister—"

"She is not a pretty little brat!"

He pursed his lips. "Perhaps you women judge differently. I'd have said she was very pretty. Whereas you, of course, are maddeningly beautiful."

Ready with an impassioned rejoinder, Valentina was thrown quite off-stride, and said in some confusion, "Oh. Well, for your information, sir, there are several noblemen at our party, so I'll get back to it at—" She stopped as his hands gripped her arms bruisingly.

"At—your—*what*?" he demanded in a growl of a voice.

"At our party. Isn't that why you came?"

"Damn and blast but it's not! What the *devil* have you been about?"

"Do not swear! Charles! You're hurting me!"

"I ought to strangle you!" His eyes murderous, he said, "You've plotted with my mother, is that it?" When her only response was to stare at him in mute astonishment, he ground out an oath. All but flinging her from him, he swung around so suddenly that his horse shied in fright and eluding the hand that grabbed for the reins, ran off.

De Michel swore again and began to sprint towards the house.

Alarmed, Valentina abandoned decorum and ran after him. "Charles—wait! What do you mean to do?"

His answer, brief and ominous, was flung over his shoulder. "You'll see!"

CHAPTER EIGHT

"IT HAS NOTHING TO DO with your present circumstances." Miss Abigail Tembury glanced uneasily around the empty entrance hall and went on, "Papa simply feels that you are too young to be forming a permanent attachment."

"Too young," said Ashford, with a derisive snort. "My mama was betrothed at seventeen, wed at eighteen and Lincoln was born before she was nineteen!"

Her fair and gentle face troubled, Miss Tembury leaned back against the bench and straightened a fold in her primrose gown. She said hesitantly, "Perhaps your papa was more settled in—his ways when they married."

"What you really mean," he riposted with a belligerence foreign to his usual good humour, "is that he had more lettuce in his bowl."

Offended, the girl stood. "I do not mean that at all, Mr. Ashford. But I think *you* have been too often to the bowl this evening."

He sprang up. "So now I'm foxed as well as an infant pauper! A pretty bobbery, by Jove! To have been rejected before I even offered! Your father takes a deal too much for granted, is what it is!"

"He did not reject you, and do for goodness' sake lower your voice. Your attentions have been most particular, and Papa merely cautioned me against—"

"Against my partiality being remarked? Against having your name spoken in connection with mine? Well I'll have you know ma'am, that I've nothing to bl-blush for 's far as my birth is concerned. My family can give yours a good two hundred years, and your papa knows it! If I was rich he would fall on my neck and—"

"I think you have said quite enough." The girl started away.

He gripped her arm. He was swaying a little, his eyes sullen and angry.

"Let me go!" she demanded. "Ashford, you are intoxicated!"

Releasing her, he said, "I may be a li'l boozy. But soon—*very* soon I'll come 'n shake a moneybag under your papa's nose, an' then you'll see him change his t-tune."

He left her and stamped an erratic path across the hall, almost colliding with the man who stalked in, booted and spurred and dressed for the road, an agitated footman trotting after him.

"Where the devil are you off to?" demanded de Michel.

"To hell!" Ashford took the stairs two at a time, and promptly tripped. He dragged himself up, and, cursing under his breath, continued on his way.

Tears glinting on her lashes, Miss Tembury fled.

The footman, outraged, informed de Michel that this was an invitational and, "if Monsieur will but wait 'ere, 'is card it shall be carried to—"

"Damn you, be still!" said de Michel thunderously. "Why should I have a card sent in to my own house?"

The footman halted but persisted bravely, "But Monsieur 'e is not *dressed!*"

"I'm sufficiently dressed for this fiasco," muttered de Michel darkly, flinging open the drawing room doors.

Breathless, Valentina sped across the hall and seized him by the arm. "Charles! I—I do not—understand. If you resent our party—"

He detached her hand. "Madam, I curst well more than *resent* it! I'm here to *end* it!"

She clutched his coat. "But—why? Why send the new furnishings if—"

Glancing around the crowded and refurbished room, he said an appalled, "Good God! Had I sent you new furnishings, Miss Ashford, which I most certainly did not, I'd have selected items suitable for a country house. Not elegancies better fitted for Versailles! More of my mother's work unless I mistake it. Now—let me be, woman!"

They had been observed, and heads were turning, a small circle of silence spreading.

De Michel cut a straight and relentless swath through the throng, the guests falling back before him, the silence deepening so that the efforts of the musicians could at last be heard.

Madame Ruth was seated on the new settee between two military gentlemen. She was laughing, her brilliant eyes peeping coquettishly over her fan.

The major at Madame's left side turned and scanned de Michel curiously.

"Maman!" The single word, uttered in a voice sharp with anger, rang through the room.

Madame Ruth's hand jerked as though she had been struck, and the wineglass she held toppled to the floor. Her widening eyes flew to meet her son's. She whispered a soundless, "Charles!"

"It is past your bedtime," said de Michel.

"No it is not," argued Madame, pale but defiant. "Go away, Charles."

The colonel at Madame's right, rose to his feet. "Now that's plain enough, sir," he said, his heavy eyebrows threatening.

De Michel's dark gaze flickered over him disinterestedly, then returned to his parent. "You are being very naughty, my dear. You know your doctor warned you about parties and excitements."

"You are ridiculous!" she snapped, adding through her teeth, "Charles—people are *staring!*"

All chin and disdain, the major rose. "Your mama says she don't want to go, de Michel."

"I'd suggest you respect her wishes, sir," said the colonel. "Or—"

"Or you will throw me out of my own house?" jeered de Michel.

The major looked dismayed. "Oh—er, haw!" he said.

"Of course," said de Michel reasonably. "If you gentlemen are willing to accept the responsibility and care for my mother should she go off in a faint again—as she did the last time she became too excited . . ."

"Er—well, egad!" mumbled the colonel, retreating a step.

"Charles!" hissed Madame Ruth, livid.

De Michel turned to her, his face cold and closed. "We do not want to create a scene, do we, *Maman?*"

For a moment her blazing eyes challenged his icy ones. Then, with a muffled sob she snatched up her fan and made her way rapidly through the fascinated guests.

Following, de Michel halted an instant, his gaze fixed on the mantelpiece where stood the portrait his mother had made of the Misses Ashford. Then, he stalked on.

In the hall, tears overflowing, Madame Ruth rushed into Valentina's ready arms. "I have . . . never . . . been so humiliated," she sobbed.

Over her shoulder, Valentina looked with disgust at de Michel. "I hope you are proud of yourself, cousin! For once, she was having a happy time. You could not bear that, could you?"

"No more than I can bear to allow you to continue to dwell here," he said acidly. "I shall require you to remove before the end of the month. Good night, Miss Ashford!"

Stunned, Valentina stared at him.

Lord Stane, dressed for the road, ushered Sidonie through the front door, and the girl called merrily, "Only see who I found Aunt, when I took your—"

She broke off, becoming aware that Madame was weeping and that her sister looked white and shocked. "Mercy!" she cried. "Whatever has happened?"

His lordship's glance took in the many interested faces in the drawing room. In a low tense voice he exclaimed, "Charles, are you gone mad?"

"*Assurement,*" said de Michel. "Come, *Maman.*"

"I will not," sobbed his mother. "Be unkind to—to me, if you m-must. But—but why vent your spleen on the poor Ashfords?"

Sidonie said uneasily, "What does she mean? Tina? What has Cousin Charles done to us now?"

"Must I carry you, madam?" asked de Michel, the grim set to his jaw leaving no doubt but that he was prepared to do so.

Watching him in dulled misery, Valentina said, "You forget yourself, cousin! This lady is—"

"Is keeping me waiting, and I've no time to waste." He took his mother's elbow. Weeping, Ruth de Michel capitulated, and tottered along beside him.

Stane moved quickly to the drawing room and closed the double doors on the curious.

"Dearest," said Sidonie. "Whatever has happened?"

"It seems that—that Cousin Charles was displeased by our party," said Valentina, her lips stiff and uncooperative. "We are given two weeks to vacate the premises."

Sidonie uttered a wail, and Stane came swiftly to take the hand she instinctively stretched out to him. "I must go," he said in his quiet way. "But pray do not be distressed, ma'am. Charles tends to speak roughly when he is angered, but he is the best of men and would never—"

"He is vile," flared Sidonie, blinking tearful eyes at him. "How can you defend a monster who treats his own mother without a vestige of kindness?"

Shocked, he protested, "No really, you must not say such things. Charles has—I mean there are things you cannot know.

"I know he has put us out of our home. And instead of comforting me, all you can do is follow your brutal bosom bow! You've an odd sense of what constitutes devotion, my lord."

The young peer glanced at Valentina and flushed guiltily. "You know my feelings for you, Miss Sidonie," he argued gruffly. "I promise you I will come back as quickly as I can, but—"

"But you mean to leave me in my hour of need," cried the beauty hysterically. "There can be no doubt where your true loyalties lie. Well, if you run to *him* you need not bother to return to me, sir. Not ever again!"

Suddenly, his amiable young face was unwontedly austere. He said coolly, "I do not care for ultimatums, Miss Sidonie."

Valentina pressed her sister's hand. "Sid, you place Lord Stane in a most difficult position."

"Not so. I allow his lordship to choose which loyalty is most valued by him. That should be simple enough, surely?"

Stane watched the girl steadily. With her head held high, her cheeks flushed, her eyes bright with anger, she was heart-stoppingly lovely. He said, "I hope you do not mean that, ma'am." He reached for her hand, but she snatched it away and turned her back to him. Pale and stern, he bowed to Valentina and was gone.

"Oh!" cried Sidonie whirling around as the door closed behind him. "Oh, hateful! All his adoration was so much hot air! Men!"

Struggling not to reveal her own conviction that she would be much better off in her grave, Valentina mumbled, "Stane worships you. And he is a fine man. You were not very wise, dearest."

"That was all I needed to hear," cried the girl tearfully. "*He* lied to and deceived me! And my own *sister* censures me, when I try to defend us!"

"I didn't mean to." Distracted, Valentina pressed a hand to her throbbing temple. "I'm sorry if—"

But Sidonie was already running up the stairs, wailing the time-honoured complaint of oppressed youth. "Nobody cares about me in this house!"

Valentina looked after her. Sidonie was only seventeen, and in the throes of her first real love. The poor child was all nerves. She must go after her. But heaven knows what their guests must think, and dear Aunt Clara was abandoned in the drawing room, doubtless feeling hopelessly besieged.

There came the unwanted memory of a pair of icy dark eyes, a contemptuously sneering mouth, a harsh voice that said with ruthless finality, "I shall require you to remove before the end of the month...." The hurt was so deep that a tiny sound of pain escaped her and she had to close her eyes for a second. Then, she took a deep breath, and walked quickly to the drawing room.

"I TOLD YOU I would not meet you again." Sidonie straightened her cloak while fixing Sir Derwent Locks with a darkling look. "And if I'd thought you were going to do that, I most certainly would not have come!"

Locks' faintly satirical smile was not pleasant, but was fortunately hidden by the shadows in this dilapidated little summer house in the Wyenott Towers rose gardens. 'Prudish little fool,' he thought. But she was a beautiful little fool and he meant to have her, so he feigned repentance. "I waited so long, my dear, and I began to despair of your coming. Then, to see you! And looking so exquisite! My sternest resolves were swept away. Forgive, I beg you. I am only grateful that you changed your mind."

"Well, I wouldn't have," she said with mournful naïvete. "Only, I needed a friend, and you *did* say you wanted to be my friend, didn't you, sir?"

"I did indeed. And have brought you something to prove it."

"Thank you," she said, her mind on weightier matters. "You see, I am in great trouble."

He looked at her uneasily. "You are?"

"We all are! Oh, Sir Derwent!" She touched his sleeve, her great eyes filling with tears. "My Cousin Charles is—is going to have us put out of our home! Only because my Aunt Ruth gave a party at the Towers!"

If there was one thing Derwent Locks could not stand, it was to see a woman blubbering. Jennifer had always been weeping about something or other. The slightest slap would bring her to tears. He thoroughly disliked being reminded of the wife who had escaped him. Only his hatred for Charles de Michel enabled him to overcome his revulsion, and dry Miss Sidonie's eyes while saying indignantly, "Good heavens! If ever I heard of such infamy! What poor Madame de Michel suffers at the hands of her crude son is not to be thought of! And now he has turned on the fairest flower in all this County!"

'My lord Stane,' thought Sidonie with a little sniff, 'might be young and good-looking, but he would do well to take lessons from this gentleman.'

She had not protested when he possessed himself of her hand. Encouraged, Locks went on, "But you must allow me to help." His arm crept about her shoulders. "I'm sure there must be a suitable house somewhere on my estate."

It had been a mistake to think of Stane. Turning her head dreamily, Sidonie encountered not his lordship's clean-cut profile and honest blue eyes, but another, considerably less clean-cut face. Locks' cheek was close to hers. His smile seemed more a leer, and there was a glow in the small deep-set eyes that she could not like. Suddenly, she felt contaminated by this man who was old enough to be her father. "Thank you, but that must be my brother's decision, of course," she said, pulling away. "Now I really must be going or I'll be missed."

He was wise enough to draw back at once. Pulling a small box from his pocket, he teased, "Don't you want to see what I promised you?"

Sidonie eyed the box uneasily. "Er...well..."

"It is just a little lovely thing. For a little lovely thing." He put the box into her hands. "A small token of my friendship, merely."

It was wrong to accept gifts from a gentleman to whom one was not betrothed or related. But how could she refuse, when he offered his help and friendship? She could at least look at it, and if it was outrageously expensive she'd have an excuse to refuse his gift.

She unfolded the silver paper and opened the small box. Inside was a charming little brooch fashioned in the shape of a cat, with emerald eyes.

"Oh, how pretty!" she cried, holding it up to the moonlight. "Good gracious! It is gold, I think."

He said theatrically, "A few moments with you are worth more than jewels to me." But the words were an unfortunate reminder, and he scowled.

This time, Sidonie did see that changed expression. "You are thinking of that wretched highwayman! Did you suffer a very great loss?"

"Very," he said through his teeth. "If I'd had my pistol with me on Thursday night, that slimy rank rider wouldn't have made off so easily!"

"I marvel they haven't caught him. He seems to be so very active of late. Have the soldiers never come near him?"

"They came near enough last week. One would think they could have run him down. Or shot him down. But the dolts whined that he has a very fast horse. I'll own it looked fast, by what I could see of it. A big black, and well-trained. Must have cost the swine a pretty penny."

Sidonie giggled. "Charles has a black Thorough-bred." She clapped her hands. "Oh, would that not be delicious? I recollect Valentina saying once that she chanced to see him very late one night, riding like the wind! How I would laugh if the mighty Charles de Michel should turn out to be a common highway-man! Only think," she went on, avidly enlarging her drama. "*That* could be the reason why he keeps his poor mama practically a prisoner! She knows his evil secret! Very likely he had planned to ride about his nefarious pursuits this very night, and he feared she might betray him at our party!" Laughing, she glanced at her companion. Her laughter died.

Locks' face held an expression of gloating triumph. He sprang up, seized her hand and bent to press his lips to her fingertips. "I salute you, fair one! But now, you will forgive me? I must ride at once!"

Bewildered, Sidonie held out the little brooch. "I cannot accept this."

Ignoring her, he all but ran to his horse, swung into the saddle, and rode off at the gallop.

Sidonie glanced up at the three-quarter moon. "I'll tell you what it is, Mr. Moon," she said. "The whole world is gone mad tonight!"

LORD SAMUEL STANE was sitting on the top step of the terrace, gazing up at the moon when the dining room door opened. De Michel came out of the cottage, sat beside his friend, and said wearily, "So you stayed. That was good of you, Sam."

Stane proffered a cigarillo, but de Michel shook his head and began to fill the bowl of his dragon's head pipe.

Stane asked, "How is she?"

"Sleeping. Wore herself out, poor soul."

Watching him, Stane handed over his tinder box, and when the light flared briefly, murmured, "She marked you, old boy."

De Michel touched the scratches on his cheek. "Yes."

"Charles, what the devil do you mean to do?"

"Get rid of the Ashfords. I ought never have let them come." He sighed, and said broodingly, "Stupid." And after a silent moment, "I think the game's up, Sam. That fellow Card has me, I suspect."

Stane had the same thought, but said supportively, "He seems scarce able to tear his eyes from your mama. If he's deep in love with her, perhaps he'll say nothing."

"He's more likely deep in love with a promotion. Looks the type." De Michel puffed on his pipe, sent up three smoke rings, then asked, "What of you, old fellow? Are you quite besotted with Miss Sidonie?"

"Quite. You don't approve, I see."

"You know better than to expect me to be tactful. She's a selfish child; in love with her own beauty and using it to get what she wants. She'll lead you a merry dance, and you're too good a man to caper to her tune."

Stane did not speak at once. Then he said slowly, "You see only the child, dear boy. I see the woman. There's a lot of her sister in her."

De Michel sat very still for a moment, then took the pipe from between his teeth and stared at it. "Then why not pay your addresses to the sister? I'll go bail she would deal more kindly with you."

"Oh, no," murmured his lordship.

De Michel's head jerked up. He demanded fiercely, "What the devil d'you mean by that?"

"Pray do not garotte me and throw my corpse to the hounds," said Stane, laughing. "Charles you gudgeon, do you fancy me a blind simpleton?"

De Michel reddened. "Not blind, at all events."

"A fellow would have to be, not to realize you are—"

"We do not discuss my situation, which is quite hopeless."

"She is no simpering ingenue. Perhaps, were you to explain matters . . ."

De Michel laughed; a short mirthless sound that made his friend wince. "Have done with your nonsense, Sam. Has your lovely child indicated an affection for you?"

"She had. Until tonight, that is."

"My apologies. That scene was ill-timed, I fear. Still, if she really cares for you, she'll get over it. Shall you speak to Ashford then?"

"Yes. But if he gives me leave to pay my addresses—"

"Hah! I wish I may see that young pauper turn away a wealthy peer!"

"—it will be a long betrothal. She is too young, too inexperienced. I believe there is kindness and compassion under her baby tantrums, and a great capacity for love. I think I can master her. I know I'm not a handsome, stormy fellow like you, stirring all the women to a flame." He threw up one arm, chuckling, as his friend hit out at him. "But I've seen what I want," he finished. "I'm willing to wait until I can claim it."

"Speaking of which," said de Michel after a brief pause. "Had you a tryst with her tonight?"

"No. When I heard about the party, I rode over to see if you'd taken leave of your senses. I met Miss Sidonie as she was returning to the house."

"Hmm," said de Michel. "Off on one of her famous strolls, was she? It runs in the family you know. You'll have to break her of it."

"Idiot. She'd gone in search of their man, Horace. I think she'd a letter wanted taking to the village to catch the night mail."

De Michel sprang to his feet and stared down at him in horror. "The night mail! My God, what a fool I am! Outmanoeuvred even while I was congratulating myself I'd been quick enough this time!"

He was down the steps in a swift leap, and running for the stables.

Sprinting after him, Stane gasped, "You cannot be sure! Man—don't be a fool. If Card really does suspect you, they'll be waiting! He'll have you!"

"They'll need fast horses!" Slowing his steps, de Michel turned into the stableyard and strode rapidly to a stall where a tall black horse came snorting to greet him. "Fetch my saddle, there's a good fellow," he said in a low voice. "The black one, Sam, and the

holsters." He led out the beautiful Thoroughbred.
"Come on Nightwind. We've business, you and I."

Stane came back hauling the saddle. He watched de
Michel throw it over the blanket, then position the
holsters and said worriedly, "They'll have extra guards
tonight, I'll wager. Charles, I'm riding with you!"

"No! I need you here. Stay with her, please Sam.
Guard her for me."

My lord Stane grumbled and swore, but agreed, and
watched as de Michel rode out and within seconds had
brought the big black to a full gallop.

'At least,' thought his lordship glumly, 'Nightwind
is very fast, and very well-trained.' But he went back
into the cottage shaking his head.

"Thank the good Lord, it is over," said Lady Clara
wearily. "At least they had the courtesy to leave early.
Did ever you see such a fiasco? The County can gossip for weeks on the events of this night!"

The imported servants were busily packing up their
supplies, watched by Horace, who hovered about,
alert lest anything belonging to his family should be
"accidentally" carried off with the caterers' goods.
The two ladies climbed the stairs, knowing that their
faithful retainer would not seek his bed until everyone had left and the house was closed for the night.

"I think there were more military than County at
our infamous party," said Valentina. "Aunt Ruth,
poor soul, is so very patriotic."

Short of breath, my lady paused on the landing. She
started a response, but one keen glance at her niece

dissuaded her, and she said instead, "Child, you look worn to a shade. Get to your bed."

When Valentina was alone in her bedchamber, she did indeed get to her bed but sat on it rather than making any move to shed her party finery. Her mind was dulled, yet supplied a stream of cameo-like impressions that came and went with amazing clarity and speed; as if a breeze riffled the pages of a picture book so that one barely glimpsed a scene before it was supplanted by another.

Her first encounter with Charles, and his white-faced fury when she had played what she'd believed to have been her trump card; the echo of his contemptuous words: "Have you ever heard of an ugly procedure called blackmail...?" Madame Ruth's sad face as she'd said, "You must not be thinking him a despot..." Sir Derwent Locks, and his grim warning, "...keep a pistol always within reach, Miss Ashford!" Charles in the scullery, soaked, shaking his smashed quizzing glass under Leslie's nose, and trying to keep his mouth stern as he'd declared, "...your family is an unmitigated disaster!" The happy rounders game, when he had seemed so warm, so kind. She shivered to the recollection of his outrageous behaviour at the top of the quarry when she'd taken him the plants. The kiss that had been so searing...so dear. And in bitter contrast, his savage rage tonight. "I shall require you to remove before the end of the month."

She had thought once that he was an enigma. It now became obvious that there was more to it than that. It could not be normal for anyone's moods to swing so erratically. The only conclusion must be that his mind was sadly disordered.

Sighing, she closed her eyes. "A certain pretty bauble in the dragon's lair..." She frowned. Who had said that? Sidonie, the day they were weeding the front garden. Sidonie. Good gracious, she must look in on her little sister; the poor girl had been so distraught. She stood, and went to the door. "A certain pretty bauble in the dragon's lair..." Sid had been speaking of Ashford's room. He'd not been present during the nightmare ending to their party, but had seemed to be enjoying himself earlier; if anything, he'd been a little too merry, and the champagne had been extreme potent. Turning down the corridor toward her sister's room, Valentina thought that Ashford must have gone to the Vicarage. She paused, frowning a little. No. The Vicar and his family had left just after Charles had dragged his mother away. She distinctly remembered that Miss Tembury had looked as if she'd been crying. Perhaps the young lovers had quarrelled. Good heavens, but this had been a disastrous party!

"A certain pretty bauble..."

She stood very still. Ashford had fallen into the habit of staying at the Vicarage very late, so that he was often sleepy the next morning. Horace had said he was "burning the candle at both ends." And it had seemed to her that her brother was not quite his usual cheerful self. She'd taken it for granted that his flirtation with Miss Tembury was not running smoothly. Suppose there was another reason... Suppose— She closed her mind to such nonsense. But she also went first to her brother's bedchamber.

There was no response to her knock. She turned the handle gently and peeped in. The lamp on the chest of drawers was turned very low. The bedcurtains were still tied back, the nightshirt lying neatly as Horace had left it.

It was silly, but she was frightened now. She went inside and glanced about. Untidy, as usual. "A certain pretty bauble…" Searching, she felt ashamed and stupid to harbour such dreadful suspicions, but she persevered. The first and most logical place would be under the mattress. She gave a sigh of relief when her difficult search revealed nothing untoward. Nor was there anything under the clothes in the chest of drawers or the highboy. She glanced at the bookcase. No, that was too obvious. Still—to be certain….

Her questing hand found nothing on the middle and lower shelves. She had to remove some volumes to reach behind the top row. She touched something soft. Her heart gave a painful jolt. She pulled out a piece of black cloth. Just an old polishing rag, probably. She held it up, and gave a little cry of shock. The eye-holes were unmistakable. With trembling hands, she took down more volumes and discovered three fat cloth bags. They were all heavy. Hoping against hope she carried them to the bed, untied the strings, and emptied out the first bag, then stood numbed with horror. She felt the rush of air as the door opened again, but could not turn around.

Sidonie said, "Oh. I beg your pardon, Valentina. I thought—" The stiffly formal words ceased. "Why do you not look at— Aah! My God!"

The terrified exclamation released Valentina from her stupor. She turned and looked at her sister. A distant corner of her mind wondered where she had been, but at this moment it seemed of small importance.

Sidonie crept to the bed. Her shaking hand took up the necklace and the room became speckled with fiery flashes of colour. "D-diamonds...?" she faltered. "Where—on earth...?"

Without a word, Valentina held up the mask.

Sidonie shrieked. "*Ashford?* My brother is The G-Galloping Gent?"

"I fear so," said Valentina, trying to be calm. "I—I think these must be...the Locks diamonds."

Her sister turned wide, uncomprehending eyes. "But—but Charles and Lady Locks st-stole them."

"No, dear. Lady Locks came to see me. I said nothing because it is such an ugly story and you were so happy. I thought I'd tell you after the party." She gave her sister a brief version of what Jennifer Locks had said. "She swore to me that neither she nor Charles had stolen the diamonds. This—" she gestured to the fiery heap on the shabby old eiderdown "—would seem to bear her out."

"But—" Sidonie pressed a hand to her cheek. "I don't understand. How could—"

"Lord save us all!" Lady Clara came bustling in, fastening a voluminous scarlet dressing gown about her uncorseted self. "Now what's to do?"

From the doorway, Horace coughed and asked tentatively, "Is anything wrong, Miss Tina?"

Somehow, Valentina pulled herself together. "Have they all gone, Horace? Then you had better both come in. We seem to have much more to worry about than a disastrous party!"

Five minutes later, Lady Rustwick broke a heavy silence. "Then Charles has told the truth throughout," she muttered. "Locks put all that vicious slander about to try and ruin him."

"I reckon as he succeeded, ma'am," said Horace grimly.

Valentina took up the black mask. "We certainly know my cousin is innocent of one thing of which he was suspected."

"Oh! Oh! Oh!" screeched Sidonie. "What have I done?" She began to weep hysterically, gasping out denunciations of her "stupid folly," of her "wickedness" that now had placed her brother's life "in jeopardy."

Lady Clara marched over and shook her niece hard. "Stop your dramatics, girl! What have you done to Ashford?"

"I—I as good as t-told Sir Derwent...that Ch-Charles is The Galloping Gent," stammered the beauty through chattering teeth.

Valentina gave a gasp of terror and lost her remaining colour.

Lady Clara said sharply, "Derwent? You saw him tonight? Where may I ask?"

"In-in the summerhouse. Aunt Ruth had asked me to take something to Horace, and afterwards I de-decided to meet Sir Derwent as he'd asked. But only for a minute! Oh! Oh! To think I have betrayed my darling brother!"

"Fiddlesticks! You said you told him that *Charles* was the highwayman. I fail to see how that threatens my nephew."

"Because I told Locks that—that Charles likely means to hold up the Royal M-Mail tonight. I was only funning, but—don't you see? My brother is not here. If he really *is* the highwayman..."

Horrified, Valentina whispered, "Locks has probably warned the troopers!"

"Lotsa ifs, Miss Sidonie," said Horace stoutly. "P'raps I better saddle up my cob and go have a look around, just in case—" He paused, listening.

A door had opened somewhere. They all stood waiting breathlessly. Footsteps progressed unevenly along the hall.

Horace limped rapidly to open the door.

Leslie Ashford lurched into the room, a sack under one arm, the other hanging limply, blood dripping from his fingertips. He took in the scene and with the ghost of a grin murmured, "Treed...by God!"

"Thank heaven you're safe," cried Sidonie, rushing to throw her arms around him and help him into the room.

Lady Rustwick hurried to fill the washbowl with water and take up a towel. "You young fool! Why ever must you do so mad a thing?"

He sank onto the bed and said faintly, "Cannot sponge off Charles...forever. Thought I'd get rich... quick 'n easy."

"You crazy boy," said Valentina, easing him out of his coat. "If that was all you wanted, these diamonds should have been enough. They're worth a fortune."

He tried to smile. "Have to give 'em back, Tina. Charles ... dashed good man. Must be cleared."

"Ugh," moaned Sidonie. "His sleeve is all ... blood!"

With a weary sigh, Ashford slid to the floor and sprawled in a dead faint.

Lady Rustwick gave a scared little cry.

Sidonie squeaked with terror.

Valentina whispered, "Oh, poor darling!"

Horace said tersely, "Horses coming!"

CHAPTER NINE

BETWEEN THEM, they managed to get Ashford into bed and had fled from his room by the time Horace opened the front door in response to a thunderous assault on it.

Walking sedately down the stairs, her heart hammering a tattoo, Valentina wondered to hear the man say, "Oh, it's you, sir." She heard no reply. Just boots. Running.

De Michel met her on the landing. He was hatless, dressed as last she had seen him, but with a dark cloak flung back from one shoulder and a long, deadly looking pistol gleaming in his right hand. She stood very still, and he checked also. For perhaps five seconds they gazed at each other. And in that brief space that seemed as if cut from time, she knew at last. She loved this wild unpredictable young man. Whatever he had done, whatever he was, she loved him. She would not give herself to him if the worst things were true. Nor could she stop loving him. She thought, 'I didn't think it would be like this.' And then, very briefly, a wistful sadness came into the dark eyes, and she knew her love was returned.

He scowled then, and said gruffly, "Don't say he's not here. There's blood on your stairs."

"He is in the red bedchamber," she said, and followed as he raced past.

He flung the door open without ceremony. They had put out the lamp, but a solitary candle cast a small circle of brightness over the bed and threw the rest of the room into shadow.

De Michel wrenched back the bedclothes and his eyes darted from Ashford's haggard young face to the crimson-stained shirt. "Damned young idiot," he said without rancour. "Where's the loot?"

Ashford struggled to one elbow. "So—you know I'm The Galloping Gent."

"I know blasted well you're not! He was in business before you came into this neighbourhood. Card knows it, which may save your neck. You're a curst poacher, is what!"

Valentina stammered, "Charles! Then—then *you're* the highwayman!"

De Michel's dark eyes flickered to her. "I was, until your brother decided to share my territory." He turned to Ashford. "Come on, man, I've little time. There's a troop heading this way. I think I led them off, but Locks was with 'em, and he'll likely bring them here. Where is it?"

Ashford sighed and sank back, nodding to his sister.

Valentina pulled the sacks from under the bed.

"Now there's an original hiding place!" Impatiently, de Michel upended the sacks, spilling out a miscellany of letters, watches, rings, fobs, several bracelets, snuff boxes, a garnet necklace, and the small case that contained the Locks diamonds. Not bothering with any of it, he flipped quickly through the letters, detached one and stared at it, then thrust it at Valentina.

"Burn this. Quickly." He stuffed the other articles back into the sack, glancing up briefly as Sidonie and Lady Clara crept into the room.

Valentina snatched up the leather case. "Charles, wait! Did you know that my brother took this from—"

"No time." He shoved it into the sack and slung it over his shoulder. "Horace—clean up Mr. Ashford's horse and saddle. I'll leave my animal here. Sidonie, clean the front steps and the stairs. Hurry, there's a good girl. Ma'am, see what you can do for your witless nephew."

Without a second wasted on argument they scattered to do his bidding.

De Michel led Valentina into the hall. "I don't think they'll question your brother. If they do, he must pretend to be drunk."

"Yes, but—"

He seized her by the chin, and said in a low savage voice, "I'm a very great fool to ever have let you stay. My apologies for that."

"Charles, I don't want—"

He bent and cut off her words with a kiss so hard she thought her lips must be bruised. A flame blazed through her. She clung to him in an ecstasy of joy that banished all other sensation. She was dazed when his mouth left hers, and she leaned limply against him. For a second he still held her, gazing down into her uptilted face. His eyes were unguarded then, and re-flected anguish and such a depth of yearning tenderness that she knew it was a farewell. A terror like nothing she had ever known froze her, but before she could speak he put her from him roughly.

She seized his arm. "What are you going to do?"

"I won't have you touched by this, my beautiful umpire. If I'm caught, I am to be loathed and despised. Remember that!"

"No! Charles—what are you going to do?"

He started to run down the stairs.

"Charles!" she cried, frenziedly.

His cynical grin flashed at her from the lower hall. "Don't be daft, love," he said, and ran outside, then stuck his head back in. "And burn that damned letter, else it will hang us all!" He was gone again.

With a sob of fear, Valentina sped to the window. She only caught a brief glimpse of him; already mounted and starting away on Leslie's black, the sack slung from the pommel. She whispered, "God go with you, my very dear," then ran to burn the letter. As she held it over the flame of Ashford's candle she recognized the writing of the direction, and for just a second she paused, doubt seizing her. Then she held it until it was burning steadily and carried it to the fireplace.

Lady Clara, busily bandaging, said, "What was it?"

"I don't know." Valentina crossed to the bed. Her brother had lapsed into unconsciousness. She stared at his pale face. "Is it bad, Aunt Clara?"

"I think not. He's young, and healthy, thank the Lord. I only pray he hasn't brought death down on—"

Sidonie ran in, her eyes enormous. "A troop of soldiers just rode by at the gallop. I saw them."

Horace came thumping in, panting, "God help Mr. de Michel! They're hard after him and he doesn't stand a chance riding Mr. Leslie's tired hack."

Sick with fear, Valentina closed her eyes for an instant.

Sidonie said, "Why on earth did my cousin not take his own horse? It is very fast, so Stane told me."

"Because if they come here, Miss," explained Horace, "the troopers would wonder why Mr. Leslie's horse had been rid hard. Mr. de Michel has made it look as if his own animal tired, so he changed mounts."

Staring at Valentina, Sidonie said, "Tina—I am so sorry. So very sorry."

From not very far off came a series of sharp cracks like dry sticks snapping.

It seemed to Valentina that the walls were closing in on her. Sidonie held her hand strongly, and she clung to her sister even as she said in a thready voice, "Horace, fetch some brandy if you please." The faithful man left them and they heard his uneven tread going down the stairs.

Ashford, who had come to himself again, said quietly, "That was gunfire, I'm afraid."

Slanting a glance at Valentina's drawn white face, Lady Clara demanded, "I'll have the truth if you please, Sidonie. You said you slipped out during our infamous party, to take something to Horace. What was it?"

"A letter. Aunt Ruth wanted him to take it into the village so as to catch the night mail."

My lady turned to her other niece. "And the letter Charles had you burn?"

"I don't know if it was the same," said Valentina. "But it was addressed in her hand."

Horace came into the room clutching a decanter and looking grim. "Dragoons, my lady! A whole troop. One hack carrying double."

Her knees shaking, Valentina managed somehow to speak calmly. "We must be quick. Please do exactly as I say..."

FOR THE SECOND TIME that night Valentina was on the landing when the front door burst open. She heard Horace protesting indignantly that the family had retired, and Card's voice sharp and incisive, requiring him to "stand aside." Pulling her dressing gown tighter over her petticoats, she walked down the last flight as Colonel Card strode across the hall, Sir Derwent Locks beside him. Her eyes went past them. Two troopers were holding up Charles de Michel who sagged in their grip, head bowed.

"Cousin Charles!" She had no need to feign anxiety. "Is he hurt? Whatever has happened, Colonel?"

Locks intervened, his eyes glittering with triumph, "Your precious cousin has got his just desserts at long last! Caught red-handed! He'll swing on Tyburn tree as a common highwayman, or—"

"I think there is no need to frighten the ladies," said the colonel icily. "Bring him in here, you men. No, ma'am! I must ask that you stay away from him! I'd be obliged if the rest of your family could be woken."

Lady Clara came in, blinking sleepily. "Small need of that, sir. You have properly disturbed the household, save for Ashford who is sleeping off his potations. Why on earth—" She checked as if only now becoming aware of de Michel, who had been guided to a chair and sat hunched over, looking very much the worse for wear. "Good God! Was Charles thrown?"

Card ignored her and glanced at Sidonie who came in looking scared but lovely in her cream silk dressing gown. "If you will pray be seated, ladies."

"Well I'll not," said my lady truculently, marching over to de Michel. "If the boy's hurt—" A trooper stepped between them, and she turned on the colonel in a flame. "What the deuce do you mean by this, sir? You'll answer for such disgraceful—"

"This man held up the Royal Mail," he interrupted coldly. "We traced him here, where he apparently took a fresh horse. I make no doubt you all are thoroughly aware of the business, and warn you that you'd do well to confess your complicity."

De Michel lifted his head, and laughed shakily. "Yes, why don't you?" he sneered. "You all . . . love me so well."

Valentina's heart was wrung to see his scratched and bruised face and cut mouth. Momentarily, words failed her.

Lady Clara said sternly, "I don't know whether you have done as the colonel says, de Michel. But you have treated us shabbily. Even so, I'd not wish you in such straits. Was it necessary that you beat him, Colonel?''

"We did not, madam. We shot his horse out from under him and he came down hard. He's lucky my men shoot straight.''

"So he can have his day with the hangman,'' said Locks gloatingly.

"You—you've no proof, damn you,'' muttered de Michel.

"We have now, sir!'' A sergeant hurried in, carrying the sack. "We found this. Looks like he'd throwed it in some bushes when he was going down!''

De Michel swore under his breath.

Locks cried a triumphant, "Bravo!''

"How very dreadful...'' whispered Valentina, envisioning noose and gibbet and wondering how on earth her love could escape them.

"Oh!'' wailed Sidonie. "To have a common thief in the family!''

"Good work, Sergeant,'' said Card. "Let's have a look.''

The sack was emptied onto a table, and everyone crowded around peering curiously at the hoard of jewels and papers.

Locks stiffened and reached out. "Jupiter! That's mine!''

The colonel moved like a striking snake to intercept that clutching hand. "My regrets. This all must be held as evidence.''

"The devil you say! That case contains—er, personal effects taken from me by this ruffian when he

held up my carriage last week. I demand you return
my property immediately!''

Card's cool stare met Locks' scowl undaunted.
''Robbery of the Royal Mail is a capital offence, and
all evidence connected with this man's activities is now
the property of the crown. We will however,'' he
added, opening the jewel case, ''give you a receipt for
the contents and—''

''No, no!'' Suddenly pale, Locks tried to close the
case. ''Not necessary, my dear sir. I am content to
wait.''

''I am not, sir.'' Remorselessly, the colonel poured
out the jewels.

Several troopers exclaimed in awe.

''My heavens!'' gasped Lady Clara. ''The Locks
diamonds! But I thought—''

''You filthy hound,'' roared de Michel, leaping
from his chair and flinging himself at the cringing
baronet.

The sergeant and a trooper ran forward. It took
both of them to force de Michel's hands from Locks'
throat and hold the enraged man back. ''Blast your
eyes, Card,'' wheezed the baronet, holding his throat.
''You allowed him . . . to attack me!''

''Unless I mistake it, sir,'' said the colonel, his voice
reflecting contempt, ''Lady Rustwick is perfectly correct. These are indeed the Locks diamonds, which you
had put about were stolen some years ago by your wife
and Mr. de Michel. It is my understanding that they
were unable to prove their innocence, and were thus
ruined. It will be most interesting to see what the authorities will make of the fact that the gems were in

your possession all the time. Meanwhile, you are quite free to leave, sir.''

Lady Clara said a disgusted, ''For shame, Locks!''

''Whatever I have done,'' Locks croaked. ''I am no sneaking highwayman!''

''I called you out once,'' panted de Michel furiously. ''Next time, you unscrupulous liar, I'll shoot straighter!''

Locks glared at de Michel in mingled fear and hatred, then took himself off.

''I've no time to waste on this nonsense,'' the colonel said briskly. ''We must have Mr. Ashford down here. Fetch him, Sergeant. And clear this room of all but the family members.''

''I'd best go with him, Colonel.'' Lady Clara surged to her feet. ''My poor nephew was quite in his cups when we got him to bed, and ain't likely to be agreeable.''

Valentina held her breath and dared not look at Sidonie.

The colonel hesitated, then gave a curt nod, and troopers and my lady went out.

De Michel swayed a little, as though the fight had exhausted him, but his gaze was steady on Card.

Smiling grimly, the colonel rested one hand on his holstered pistol. ''I don't recommend it. You'd never leave the house alive.''

''Might beat hanging,'' said de Michel, but he sank wearily onto the new settee.

Card separated all the items on the table, paying particular attention to the letters. He said at length, ''There is one missing. Where is it, de Michel?''

"You have everything, *mon cher colonel*."

"I think not. There was another letter. It contained highly secret information which was—shall we say, extracted?—from a high ranking officer while he was under the influence of some drugged champagne."

This, Valentina had not expected. "Oh, heavens," she gasped, her hand flying to her throat. "Colonel, I swear we put nothing in that wine!"

"I believe I have not accused you, ma'am."

Lady Clara came back into the room. "Accused her of what, pray?"

Ashford, ghastly pale, and wearing a dark dressing gown over his nightshirt, staggered in on the sergeant's arm. "Why a'God's name must I be hauled out of m'bed of suffering," he groaned, lowering himself painfully into the nearest chair. "An' watcha saying 'bout m'sister?"

Marvelling that her brother was such a consummate actor, Valentina explained, "Colonel Card says that military secrets were—were taken during our party, dearest. He seems to believe the information was sent out in a letter that Cousin Charles—er, appropriated from the Royal Mail tonight."

Ashford blinked at her owlishly. "Aunt Clara told me 'bout the diamonds. Not 'bout the letter. 'S this fella right, Charles? You been m-messing 'bout with the High Toby?"

"With a good deal more than highway robbery." The colonel drew himself up. "However, that is a starting point, wherefore I formally accuse you, Charles de Michel, of being the rank rider known as The Galloping Gent. In every instance save the last three robberies, the items you stole were later found in the village church. I presume therefore, that the goods in this sack are the proceeds from your most recent crimes."

"You are very presumptuous, sir," drawled de Michel mockingly.

"I cannot think why the colonel should presume such stuff," said Lady Clara, mystified. "Bless my soul if I ever heard such a cockaleery tale! Why would a highwayman risk his neck to rob, and then return the spoils? He'd have to be wits to let."

"Unless," said the colonel, "his robberies were merely to cover the fact that he was in actuality removing secret documents from the mails."

"Gad! What an imagination," murmured de Michel.

Valentina said in a puzzled way, "Do you say that secret documents are being sent out from Herefordshire, Colonel Card? From some military station?"

"No, ma'am. The work of spies, not the military."

"But surely, if Mr. de Michel were sending military secrets through the mails, he would have no cause to intercept his own letters?"

"Unless," put in my lady shrewdly, "they were not *his* letters."

"Very good, ma'am," said the colonel.

"If I stole some unknown person's correspondence," said de Michel, "then that person must bring charges against me. Has anyone done so, Card?"

The colonel smiled thinly. "Sir, I've no least intention to stand here and bandy words with you. It is my personal belief that you either worked hand-in-glove

with, or were aware of the existence of an extremely
dangerous ring of spies in London. For some reason,
you parted with them, and removed here where you
thought to be far from suspicion. Certainly, we are
aware that although we were given information that
led to the arrest of the spies in Town, the ringleader
conveniently escaped.''

Valentina cried, ''Do you say that my cousin un-
masked a gang of wicked Bonapartists?''

''If that is so,'' said my lady, ''you owe the boy a
debt of gratitude!''

''*If* such a fantasy proved true, I agree, ma'am.
However, the treasonable activities have continued. It
seems obvious, therefore, that Mr. de Michel, knowing the identity and whereabouts of the ringleader,
followed him to Herefordshire, and has been stealing
the secrets the traitor sends out, intending to sell them
himself.''

Valentina was very frightened, but managed to say
admiringly, ''It sounds to me as if some very clever
work has gone on here. If your master spy slipped
away from London, Colonel, how on earth did you
trace him to Herefordshire? Or did you already suspect my cousin?''

''Not at that point in time, ma'am,'' said Card, with
a smile at the young lady who was as perceptive as she
was beautiful. ''To say truth, that was pure luck. We
chanced to find a scrap of paper at the scene of a hold-
up near here. The document was marked with the
symbol used by the London spy ring. The same mark
was on one letter in the mail sack tonight, which now
seems to have disappeared.''

De Michel said, "You have read this mysterious letter?"

"Indeed I have, and allowed it to be carried on, so that we might catch the villain for whom it was intended. It is very obvious that the information was obtained at the party in this house, and was immediately written down and sent off to London. Am I right, sir?"

"I'd say you're ripe, rather than right, Card. Ripe for Bedlam."

The colonel frowned. "Don't be a fool. I warn you I mean to have a confession and make my arrest this very night, one way or t'other."

De Michel came to his feet. He was very pale, but said laughingly, "You'll not get one from me! I have never belonged to a traitorous society. I have never stolen government secrets. You cannot prove otherwise."

Card whirled on Sidonie. "You left the party at about half-past ten o'clock, miss. Why?"

Startled, the girl said, "Well—I . . . I—"

"You will answer truthfully if you value your head! Or if you wish to prevent my suspicions turning to your brother, who likely knows more of this than he's saying!"

"Don't shout at her," gasped Ashford, struggling to get up, but sinking back again.

Card stamped closer to the shrinking girl. Towering over her, he thundered, *"Why—did—you leave? It was to send off a letter—no?"*

"It—I…" Terrified, the girl burst into tears. "Yes! But—but I do not see why my brother should be sus—"

"To whom was it directed?"

"I did not notice," she said wringing her hands distractedly.

"Could it have been to a gentleman in London, perhaps?"

Sidonie's face gave her away. She gulped out, "I d-don't know."

"To conceal evidence is to share the guilt, Miss Ashford! Who gave you the letter? Answer! Or I shall be obliged to arrest you as an accomplice!"

Sidonie threw one hand to her mouth, her eyes, wide with terror, turning in frantic appeal to her sister.

"That's enough, Card," said de Michel quietly. "Stop frightening the child. You have me. I writ the letter."

Card sneered, "So! A confession after all. Go on, sir. I'd like to know how you managed it, since you was not at the party."

De Michel said slowly, "I flatter myself that I covered my tracks well. This is my house, remember? There is a priest's hole behind the drawing room bookcases. I hid there and was able to hear all that was said. My mama, fortunately, is excessive patriotic, and makes a practice of having military men about her. I learned many facts in that way. Last night, I writ down what I heard, intending to ride to the village and send off my letter. However, my brainless little cousin was wandering about the gardens, so I gave it to her and told her to be sure it reached the Royal Mail."

Sidonie darted a shocked glance at her sister, but watching helplessly as de Michel deliberately sealed his doom, Valentina kept silent.

Card said, "You'd have done better to take it to the village yourself. But I fancy you had another matter to concern you. Yes?"

"You are most astute, sir. My mother has knowledge of some of my activities. They mean nothing to her, but were she to mention them a more shrewd mind would soon put two and two together."

"Hence your hurried and most ungallant removal of the poor lady."

De Michel bowed ironically. "Until I walked into the party I had not realized you were present. When I saw how you hung on my mother's words, I guessed you suspected me. I knew my one chance was to retrieve my letter."

"I presume you have destroyed it," said Card. "But we have the man's name and will be watching the Holborn Receiving Office."

"Without my letter, you'll have no proof."

"True. But we will have his identity. And meanwhile, we have you, sir!" The colonel turned to the silent onlookers. "The symbol these traitors used is an interesting one. I want you to look at it carefully and tell me if ever you have seen it on any other document." He pulled a notebook and pencil from his pocket and thrust them at de Michel. "Draw it."

"The devil I will! Why should I help you convict me?"

"To rob the Royal Mail is a hanging offence of itself," said Card reasonably. "What have you to lose? Unless—you are protecting somebody else."

De Michel eyed him speculatively. "If I do cooperate, will the Court be more lenient?"

"Perhaps."

Taking the notebook de Michel stared at it for a minute.

Card said softly, "You *do* know the symbol you used, sir?"

"Of course. Only—I'm a trifle shaken and my hand's not too steady."

"Just make it as approximate as possible."

Scowling, de Michel complied, and for a tense moment concentrated on what was an apparently painstaking effort. Card snatched the notebook, stared at the drawing, and looked up from under his brows. "Just as I thought."

"Not—up to par," said de Michel with a rather strained grin. "Blame yourself. You have made me nervous. I'll own it."

Valentina saw little beads of perspiration on his forehead, and the hand he put up to run through his tumbled hair was trembling.

Card set the notebook aside and drew a crumpled paper from his pocket. "And were you nervous when you drew this?" he purred.

Noticeably paler, De Michel glanced at the sketch he'd made when they had discussed his plans for the quarry garden. He said jerkily, "You've harboured your suspicions for some time, Colonel."

"And you, sir, are a liar. I let you run on with your nonsense to see how you might explain it all away. The main trouble is that you're a very poor artist. On the other hand," Card marched to the mantelpiece, and snatched up the sketch of the Ashford sisters. "This was drawn by a most skilled—"

De Michel sprang and tore the sketch from his hand. "Damn you—you'll not use that!"

The sergeant ran to assist his officer, but Card had already whipped out his pistol and now flailed it savagely.

Without a sound de Michel crumpled and lay motionless.

Valentina screamed and ran to kneel beside him. Blood was slipping down his forehead. She said fiercely, "Had you to hit him so hard?"

"I've no sympathy to waste on a highwayman," snapped the colonel. "Sergeant, I'm off to arrest de Michel's accomplice—the ringleader of the pack! Keep him under close arrest. If he escapes, you will be held responsible. Post guards at all the outer doors. There may be others coming to his aid. No one is to enter or leave until I return."

"Yussir. You don't never mean to go alone, sir?"

"Good God, man, I hope I am capable of controlling one puny woman!"

The sergeant's jaw dropped. "A *woman*, sir?"

"Regrettably. It's an ugly business. Keep alert now, there must be no mistakes." Card's keen eyes shifted to the silent onlookers. He said sternly, "I believe you people are innocent. Do not give me cause to change

my mind." Turning on his heel, he strode from the
room.

There began a wait which Valentina found as nerve-
racking as it was interminable. The sergeant, a not
unkind man, allowed de Michel to be lifted onto the
settee where Lady Clara and Valentina tended the cut
in his head. He showed no sign of recovering con-
sciousness, and the sergeant allowed that he might
never wake up. "Which would," he said cheerfully,
"be as well."

Ashford, who had been looking ever more wan,
announced at this point that he wished he'd not taken
so much champagne at the party, and was feeling "as
sick as a coach horse." With commendable alacrity the
sergeant ordered two troopers to convey "the unfortunate gentleman" to his bedchamber. Ashford reeled
off, moaning, a pale and scared Sidonie following.

Valentina begged her aunt to go up to bed, but Lady
Clara said she would wait until the colonel returned,
settled into her favourite saggy armchair, and fell
asleep almost immediately. Valentina pulled an occasional chair close to the settee and took up her vigil.
Sleep for her was out of the question, and as the weary
moments dragged past her mind sank deeper into despair. However she sought a way out, she could see no
possibility of Charles escaping the hideous death of
public hanging. He was known to have held up the
Royal Mail; not once, but several times. The fact that
he had returned most of the stolen articles was unlikely to weigh with the stern administrators of justice.
He had admitted his involvement with the spies, and
while he had evidently succeeded in circumventing

their activities, had attempted to shield the prime suspect. A sudden horrifying vision of his beloved self hanging lifeless in chains and left to rot as a warning to the populace caused her to throw her hands over her eyes and shrink, whimpering, in the chair.

She dozed briefly, and when she next looked at the clock, it showed a quarter past two. Aunt Clara was snoring softly. The sergeant had gone out, probably in search of sustenance. Her puzzled thought that Colonel Card should have come back long before now was forgotten when she saw that, although de Michel lay still, his brows were pulled into a frown of pain.

She took the cloth from the bowl beside her, and bathed his face gently. He opened haggard eyes and looked a question.

"He's not back, love," she said, her attention so fully on him that she didn't notice the door open, or hear Sidonie creep in.

De Michel murmured, "When I'm taken, send...for Stane." And searching her tired face, he pleaded, "You do...understand now?"

"Yes. You were trying, all the time, to stop her. But also, to protect her." She stroked his cheek lovingly. "Poor darling. What a pickle you were in. You must love her very much."

The ghost of a smile flickered. His voice was faint, and she could tell it pained him to talk. She judged the need greater than the penalty, and made no effort to stop him when he began to explain haltingly. "Mama worshipped my father. Wouldn't allow anyone...to do anything for him that she could possibly do herself. She loved me, but only as a reflection...of him.

But whenever I was troubled or—or ill, she was all tenderness. I caught the pneumonia when I was seven, and she...sat by me day and night for almost a week. She used to...sing to me." He stopped speaking, his lips gripped tightly together, his eyes closed again. Valentina lifted his hand and pressed a kiss on it, and said nothing.

She thought he had fallen asleep, but in a little while he sighed and went on, "After we had to fly The Terror, we came to England. My father got it into his head that people mistrusted him because he was French. He overheard someone talking about dirty Frogs once, and was sure they meant...him. He couldn't be easy until we removed to Italy. One night in Rome, he was robbed and beaten. He—he almost died. Mama was frantic. She brought him back to London, but he was never quite well again. She said it wouldn't have happened if England had been kinder. When—when he died, I think..." He frowned deeply, then blinked up at her as if reluctant to continue.

She said, "Rest easy, Charles. Tell me another time."

He said wryly, "There won't be another time, I think," and as she flinched and bowed her head, he went on, "After Papa's death, I think she became..." The words trailed off. Another pause, then he said, "She developed a deep hatred of this country. For a long time I didn't realize—how deep. She surrounded herself with military friends. I thought at first she was looking for—for a new husband. I don't know just when I began to suspect... But—when I knew she was sending information to France, I had to stop her."

His head tossed and he winced and pressed a hand to his temple. Valentina said softly, "So you managed to unmask her group of spies in Town, and you brought her down here, and kept her isolated, but still she managed to circumvent you."

"Yes, but she's not responsible. That is—I don't think she— The shock of losing Papa... Her poor mind, you know..." He seemed to suffer a sharper spasm, and had to stop and turn his head away. He finished breathlessly, "I really do love England, Tina. I tried my best."

A small sob escaped Sidonie and Valentina whirled around. She saw the glitter of tears and knew that her sister had heard this, and was glad. She whispered, "You should be asleep, dear. How is my brother?"

"Resting now. Tina..." The girl crept forward, eyeing de Michel's wan face in an awed way. "That repulsive colonel hasn't come back yet. Do you see the time?"

Valentina peered at the clock. "Ten minutes to three! Good heavens! Whatever can have happened?"

Lady Clara had also awoken and she said dryly, "I'd not put it past—"

A sudden flurry of shouts from the hall. Boots stamping closer. The door burst open, and Lord Samuel Stane, closely followed by the sergeant, came quickly into the room.

De Michel dragged himself to one elbow and looked at their sombre faces apprehensively.

The sergeant said, "See here, y'r lordship, me colonel says no one wasn't to come in nor go out! Not meaning no disrespeck, sir, but you can't come pushing in here like this!"

Stane strode past him, holding out a letter. "Your mother has gone, Charles. I fancy Colonel Card is after her. She left this for you."

De Michel blinked at the letter, then glanced at Valentina. She took the folded sheet from his lordship and broke the seal, then looked at de Michel enquiringly.

"Please..." he said.

In silence she ran her eyes swiftly down the beautifully written page:

I have beaten you, Charles! All this while you have blocked me at every turn, never caring that I fought to avenge the death of your martyred father. If you had loved me, you would have fought with—not against me. I always knew you were jealous of my great love for my husband, but I never dreamed it would lead you to undo everything I struggled so hard to achieve.

You trapped and betrayed my poor friends in London, and you thought that by imprisoning me in this wilderness, my efforts for France would be stopped. Well, I outwitted you! Colonel Card has just come for me. I know you wait there for the word that, thanks to your treachery, I am to be dragged to Town to be hanged as a spy. A bitter reward for the trusting mother who bore and cherished you!

I have outwitted you again! Herbert Card has given me his heart. He will never replace my beloved Henri, but he is comfortably circumstanced and has offered to take me to the New World. By the time you read this, we will be far beyond all threat of capture.

Farewell, my wicked son. I leave without a *soupçon* of regret, sure in the knowledge that my friend Napoleon Bonaparte will soon defeat your stupid Wellington and take full revenge upon *la perfide Albion!*

Please note that my last word to you is 'farewell.' Not goodbye, or *adieu,* both of which invoke a blessing.

It is with the fervent prayer that I never shall see you again, that I sign myself,

Ruth de Michel

Stunned, Valentina thought, 'Good heavens! He has enough to bear, without this!' and was very glad she had not read the letter aloud. She said, "Your mama and Colonel Card have—have eloped."

"What?" gasped de Michel.

"The devil," said Stane, grinning broadly.

The sergeant whispered an incredulous, "Cor luvaduck!"

"She bids you farewell," Valentina went on, holding the sheet closer to the candlelight where de Michel could not see it. "They are bound for the New World, it seems." She knew that Stane watched her intently, and with a mute look of warning handed the letter to him.

He ran his eye over it rapidly. Rage came into his face and he made as if to tear the sheet, but the sergeant's hand shot out to appropriate it.

"Evidence!" he declared, and thrust the letter into his pocket. Turning to the settee, he came to attention. "Charles de Michel," he roared formally. "I arrest you in the King's name on suspicion of high treason and robbery of the Royal Mail!"

CHAPTER TEN

London, September 23, 1813

My Dear Valentina:

I trust all is well in Herefordshire and that you and my sister and Aunt Clara go along nicely.

It has been slow going here. De Michel is still under close arrest, and even Stane was unable to get us leave to see him. (Stane, incidentally, has proved to be the best of good fellows. He has spoke to me about fixing his interest with Sidonie, but made it clear he wants a long betrothal, as he considers her too young at present for the married state. I agree, and have consented.)

Back to my cousin: We do know that he is in good spirits, so you may be easy on that score.

There was, as I wrote you, talk of a public trial. I am glad to be able to advise that this was abandoned. The authorities have decided on what they are calling an Enquiry, which is to be held tomorrow at the Horse Guards. Stane is bending every effort to get us admitted, but thus far without success.

I continue in excellent health. My arm is quite healed and don't bother me a jot. I have been to

Fives Court with Stane, and saw him spar a round with Gentleman Jackson at his rooms in Bond Street. His lordship peels well, and did jolly well too, by Jove, but he did!

There is much talk in Town about a novel called *Pride and Prejudice*, and about that strange French lady, Madame de Staël. Everyone hangs on her lips, but she strikes me as nothing out of the ordinary way.

Do you recall that odd little German who tried to interest Papa in his scheme of light and heat? Would you believe it? The chap has managed to perfect his notions, and there is a parish in Westminster that has *gas street lamps!* Stane and I went over and watched the lamplighter. It was marvellous to see, and quite a crowd following him about, and the light was fairly blinding! I am going to enquire, with Stane's help, if Papa ever did buy into this scheme. Stane says that if he did, we may become rich. (Wherefore Miss Tembury might be more polite the next time she sees me!)

I know you are anxious about poor Charles, so will post this off tonight, without waiting for the results of tomorrow's hearing.

Yr. affectionate brother,
Ashford

Postscriptum: Success! Stane just this minute returned, and we are allowed to attend the Enquiry! Will advise you tomorrow.

London, September 24, 1813

My Dear Valentina:

A great deal of news, but I've much to do and it is late, so if this letter is to catch the mail coach, must be brief.

The Enquiry was frightful. Stane said he couldn't make it out at all, as it was a trial in all but name. I am astounded that de Michel stood up under it as well as he did. The poor fellow looked worn to a shade after they fired questions at him for two hours without ceasing. He fielded them jolly well, but his interrogators were beastly shrewd and had gathered so much information against Aunt Ruth that Charles was driven to the ropes. He would say nothing against her, and at several points was obliged to refuse to answer rather than incriminate her. This did not sit well with the Court, as you may guess. He made absolutely no mention of a certain gentleman he once referred to as "A Poacher", for which I am most grateful.

Counsel for the Defence was an army colonel; a very polished old boy but with an alarmingly drowsy manner. By one o'clock, when they adjourned for luncheon, I truly thought Charles doomed. He gave us a grin, but I think he shared my conviction, and I know Stane was worried.

After luncheon they started hammering at Charles again, bringing in a string of witnesses, some of whom had been on the stagecoaches. None of them recognized the—er—"Poacher"—

thank God! But of all the ingratitude! They had not a good word to say for Charles. I can tell you they looked pretty silly when the Drowsy Counsel pointed out that all their goods had been returned. The Prosecutor was relentless however, and was arguing for the Death Penalty, and it began to looked very black indeed. Then the Drowsy Counsel stood up. Tina, I was never more astonished! The old boy had become a ravening tiger! He based his defence on the fact that Charles had tried desperately to be true to England, while protecting his mother, whom he loved deeply. He was so eloquent and convincing I think there was scarce a man there but was not won over. His most telling point was made when he produced that dreadful letter Aunt Ruth writ to Charles, and read it aloud. It was very evident Charles had known nothing of it, and it hit him very hard. He turned perfectly white, and I hope I may never again see a man look so stunned. When the colonel finished you could literally have heard a pin drop. I think Charles would prefer I not tell you this, but I saw tears on the poor fellow's cheeks. He quickly pretended to blow his nose and removed the evidence, but I believe the members of the Court had seen also. It was the *coup de grace* for the Prosecution.

Charles was chastised quite sternly for turning highwayman to reclaim his mother's treasonable letters and for not having at once taken his knowledge of spying activities to the Horse Guards, but was then thanked for his efforts in behalf of England.

He is set free, Tina! I fancy you will be seeing him back in Herefordshire very soon.

Tomorrow, I shall look into the matter of what they are now calling The Gas, Light and Coke Company.

I know this letter will have brought you welcome news. I share your happiness. He is an honourable gentleman and one I am proud to call cousin. (Though I wonder if I may soon call him brother-in-law...?)

> Yr. devoted brother,
> Leslie Ashford

With the Light Division

France, November 8, 1813

Dear Miss Ashford:

You will be thinking me a proper rudesby not to have come to see you before I left England. The circumstances under which we met, and under which we parted, seemed to me to forbid that I approach you in any way.

You must know, in view of what has passed between us, that I had hoped to make you my wife. It was a dishonourable ambition. I knew of the disgrace that shadowed my name, but, like a perfect fool, hoped I could contrive to smooth everything over. I should have realized that the rumours Sir Derwent Locks spread about me had already caused sufficient scandal that I should not ask a lady of Quality to ally herself with me.

You will know that I have bought a commis-

sion and am now Lieutenant de Michel. I find a
soldier's life much less exciting than I had supposed. It offers a grand reward, however; two in
fact. Firstly, I can delude myself into thinking I
am at last really doing something for my country. (Whereas the truth is that I am an almost in-
distinguishable cog in a very large wheel).
Secondly, dear old Stane seems to have wrote to
my colonel, whose father was at Eton with Stane's
sire. Sam must have told the most awful lies, because instead of being regarded as a "Dirty
Frog", as I had fully expected, I find myself
lionized as some sort of intrepid Intelligence officer, who single-handedly defended Britain
against a horde of dastardly spies. I thought this
highly diverting at first, but alas, there is a price
on everything: now, I am expected to live up to
my reputation!

We are told that tomorrow we are in for a major battle. I have seemed to bear a charmed life
thus far, but I thought it as well to warn you that
in case my existence should be cut short, I have
made provision for you to inherit the entire estate of Wyenott Towers (which is not entailed). I
made only one stipulation, which is that for the
duration of her life, my mother be allowed to occupy the Steward's Cottage on the estate whenever it is her desire to do so. I have ordered my
Town house sold, the proceeds to be paid into an
account which shall be at your disposal. No, do
not cavil, Sweet Umpire. You cannot maintain the
Towers and complete our Quarry Garden without funds.

I must tell you that I have had the pleasure of meeting my Cousin Lincoln. Due to the positions of our regiments we encounter one another seldom, but we struck up quite a friendship. I am pleased by his deep affection for you. The family resemblance is so strong, however, that it is as well for my peace of mind he is not to be met with every day.

I hope Sidonie does marry Stane. He is a capital fellow and has loved her, I believe, from the moment he first saw her. I rather doubt that Ashford will wed little Abby Tembury; at least, not for some years. As for Miss Ashford herself—my dear, how blessed the man who will call you wife. How very much I longed to do so. But I fancy that priceless reward will go to a worthier and less notorious gentleman than myself.

I write this hearing the gunfire from some distant skirmish, and with my thoughts on the quarry. Details seem oddly vivid tonight. I have the strongest conviction that you will complete the garden and make of it something truly beautiful. If you do, will you sometimes open it to the public so that others can enjoy it? But just occasionally, when you walk there, I hope you might think of the fellow who had little to recommend him, but who carried your picture in his heart to the end of his days, and signs himself, truly,

> Ever yours,
> Charles de Michel

France, November 13, 1813

My dear brother:

Well, we have had a great victory, as you will certainly be aware by the time this letter reaches you. It was a hard-fought struggle and old Soult gave us a run for our money. I will set your mind at ease, Leslie, and say that I am unscathed. Further, since poor Freehampton was killed, I have got my Company, and my Captaincy!

You will hear of several nigh incredible incidents which occurred during the battle. *Nota bene,* Col. Colborne bamboozled a large French garrison into thinking themselves surrounded, so that they surrendered, not realizing it was instead Colborne's regiment which was outnumbered! As grand a piece of trickery as ever I heard. You may also be proud of our cousin de Michel, who led a troop into enemy lines to cover the retreat of one of our gun carriages which had got itself cut off. When his sergeant was brought down in the thick of it and his hack killed, Charles dismounted under heavy enemy fire and hoist the sergeant across his own horse. Unfortunately, before he was able to mount up again, he was hit, but sent the horse off. His man and the gun crew were saved. I am most sorry to relate that de Michel is listed missing, believed killed. They say he will be mentioned in despatches for conspicuous gallantry. I rather doubt it, for Old Nosey is famous for failing to reward valour. Do you know that in spite of the superb conduct of Colborne's 52nd, Wellington's only comment was to rake Colborne down because his fellows commandeered some chickens for their dinner! At all events, de Michel was a dashed fine gentleman and no matter the rumours about him, I'm proud to claim kinship.

I think your letters are not getting to me, for I have heard no more of the interesting development between Stane and my little sister. Shall we have a baroness in the family? Do write soon and ease my heart-burnings over this!

The rain is invading my poor hut, which seems likely to collapse, so I must close in haste, sending my love to all,

Lincoln Ashford, (*Captain!*)

"THEY WANT ME TO ACCEPT that he is dead, Fitz." Valentina lifted the box of cuttings from one of the panniers slung across the donkey's back. She carried it to the fourth step where she set it down, and paused to survey the results of her labours. So often during the dark and endless sixteen months since Lincoln's letter had come, she had worked here. Ashford had helped her until the dividends from Papa's shares in The Gas, Light and Coke Company had enabled him to realize his dream of a commission in the Navy. Sidonie and Horace had laboured long hours at the quarry, and even Lord Sam had come whenever he could get away from his own estates, or when he had no business to attend to in the House of Lords. A conscientious young peer, Lord Sam, and would make Sidonie a good husband, just as Charles had said.

Charles... The familiar pang jagged through her heart and she closed her eyes for a moment. 'Dear Lord, please—let him come back to me. I am probably foolish, Lord, to keep on hoping. But I won't give up. I won't!'

The chill wind tugged at her bonnet. She straightened it abstractedly. March was almost over. The second March since he had gone from her. Crocus were peeping up here and there, and snowdrops were lifting their bright little faces to the pale sun. The mosses had taken hold nicely and were already softening the jagged rocks beside the steps. Far below, the young lawns were vividly green. The trees Horace and Lord Sam had planted near the area that someday would be the lake, looked spindly and forlorn, but at least they had not died. Despite all their efforts, the changes were so small as yet, but they gave a hint of how it would look eventually. And when summertime came there would be more blossoms and it would be brighter. If Charles was not home by then, she would have to accept his death. She bit her lip, and knelt, digging angrily at the damp earth.

If he dared show his face here, she'd give him a piece of her mind! To let her worry so! Not a letter; not a line; not even a message in all this time! Beastly creature! He wouldn't deserve so much as a word, much less—

Only—if he *didn't* come... She sat back on her heels and stared blankly at the little hole she had dug. If he didn't come there would be nothing in life.... No, that wasn't true. She had her dear family. Soon now, Sidonie and Lord Sam would marry and set up their

nursery, and she would be an aunt, but there would be
no marriage for Miss Valentina Ashford; no children
of her own. Charles had so loved children.... Still, she
would have a task to occupy her, for the Quarry Garden must be made just as he had hoped—a thing of
beauty where man's greed had made ugliness. If she
achieved that as his memorial, she would—

FitzMoke brayed loudly, and Valentina jumped.

A deep voice said, "There's little wonder so much
remains to be done, Miss Ashford! I vow you move so
fast as any snail!"

Her breath was snatched away, and her heart gave
such a gigantic leap that she was dizzied. With a sob
she jerked her head up, to stare at the man who stood
at the top of the quarry watching her and caressing the
little donkey.

He wore his uniform, and had changed. He was
thinner, and his carriage was slightly different. All this
she saw in the first frozen seconds. Then her eyes
blurred because with his free hand he was leaning
heavily on a cane.

She did not seem to move, yet the cane had been
thrown aside, his arms flung wide, and she was clasped
tight against his heart. Neither spoke, nor did they
make any attempt to do more than cling to each other
through that first ecstatic moment. Valentina found
then that she was weeping and whispering thanks for
this answer to her prayers. De Michel, his cheek
pressed against her silken hair, his eyes closed, murmured, "My Tina. My Lovely Little Umpire... At
last! At last!"

"At last, is it?" She drew back, trying to frown at him through her happy tears. "Where have you been, wretched man? Why did you not at least let me know you were alive? Do you know how I have wept and worried and—"

His lips silenced her. His kiss was not quite as hard, his arms not quite as crushing as she remembered, but the embrace was so precious that she felt awed by the joy of it. He stumbled slightly, and she flew to take up his cane and walk with him, FitzMoke thudding patiently along behind them.

Their progress was slow, their route erratic, but neither noticed, for they seemed to float along, arms about each other. When they came to an oak tree with obliging roots, they sat down close together. Valentina was full of anxious questions, and de Michel told her about the kindness of the French *Capitaine* who had ensured he be carried to the rear after he was hit. He made light of his wound and of his long struggle to survive, but Valentina had been quick to note the new lines in his face, the shadows under the dark eyes, and was not deceived.

"So many months of pain and loneliness," she said, stroking his hollow cheek tenderly. "If I could only have been with you. But you are an officer, Charles. Surely they should have notified our forces that you were a prisoner?" Her eyes sharpened with suspicion. "Besides, the war ended after the Battle of Toulouse last April; almost a year ago! Are you still in the Army, then? Do you say you were kept in France after that?"

"Stane thought you would like to see me in this regalia, but I have sold out." He hesitated, avoiding her eyes, then admitted, "I was brought home last May, but I could not walk. They—er, thought I might never walk again."

"My poor love!" Appalled, she kissed the hand she held, but then comprehension dawned. "So *you* were the one kept the news from us! Oh! How infamous! And you meant to hide away from me forever, because of your horrid pride? If you are not the most provoking man who ever lived!"

"Now don't fly out at me, you wild woman! Jove, but you'd be a fit mate for a rank rider, be dashed if you wouldn't."

"You evidently did not think so a year ago!"

Sobering, he lowered his eyes, and said with rare humility, "No. Well, there was—that other business, you see. And—I thought how it would be for you. I mean, only think of the superb offer I could make you. Pray come and nurse a man who was branded as a highwayman and a traitor. And who is an invalid, to boot! Gad! Such honour must have fairly bowled you out!"

Between her teeth, Valentina said, "I think you are perfectly abominable! Did you fancy me so weak-kneed I would not want you because you could not walk? A fine opinion you have of me, sir!"

He groaned as she tried to pull back, and wrenched her to him once more. "I might have known I'd walk into a hornet's nest! Have you no pity for a poor soldier who comes to you crushed and broken—"

"Crushed and broken, my aunt's bonnet!" Despite her angry words, she scanned his pale face anxiously, but the gleam in the dark eyes, the betraying twitch beside the humorous mouth, reassured her. She went on with vigour: "Do not try to look pathetic, Charles de Michel! When I think of the grief and misery I have endured, never dreaming that all the time you were close by and did not care enough to even discover how I went on!"

"Of course I cared. Besides, Sam kept me informed as to—"

"Sam!" With a squeak of wrath, she pushed not too forcefully against his chest. "Let me go, you steely invalid! Sam, is it? So he *knew* you were alive! The deceitful wretch! How could he have looked into my face and seen my sorrow and not had the simple decency—"

"Because I told him not to, of course."

"Did you indeed? And how if I had gone into a decline?"

He grinned. "You are not the declining sort."

"You flatter yourself that you know all about me." She tossed her little chin up, even as that so well-remembered dauntless grin made her ache with love for him. "What presumption! And even more presumption that you should have taken it for granted I would wait for you all these months!"

"Whereas, in point of fact, you are about to wed Derwent Locks."

"If you think, Sir Smugly, that I can do no better than—"

"Oh, do be quiet," said de Michel, and enforced the command by the simple expedient of clamping his lips over hers.

When that ruthless embrace ended, he leaned back his head against the tree trunk and gasped, "Miss Ashford! Pray be so good as to exercise a little restraint. I am not a well man!"

"I wish you were," said Valentina rather dizzily. "If only so that I might scratch you!"

He laughed and pulled her to him again, and the golden moments slid by while they exchanged the caresses, the tender assurances that meant so much to both loving hearts. At length, after a time when they had said nothing at all but had not been idle, Valentina murmured, "Have you the least notion I wonder, of how your farewell letter made me weep? It *was* a farewell—no, Charles?"

He hesitated, frowning, then admitted reluctantly, "Yes. I had the strongest premonition that it would be my last battle." He shrugged, and added with a wry smile, "Fairly well justified, as it chanced."

Valentina shivered. "It was so kind in you to make the provision for your mama." She felt him tense, and went on gently, "Do you really think she will ever visit the cottage again?"

"Unless there is some kind of amnesty I very much doubt it. She must realize she will be subject to arrest if she returns to England. I suppose— Well, just in case she ever should write, I really—just wanted her to know that...that..."

"That you have not closed the door, so to speak?"

He tightened his arm about her gratefully, and nodded.

Valentina smiled and snuggled closer. "Have you realized how she tried to exonerate you, dearest? Ashford said that her last letter to you was your Counsel's *pièce de résistance* at the Enquiry. Aunt Ruth must have writ in that way because she knew it would help to clear your name."

His face expressionless, de Michel knew that if *Maman* had meant to clear his name, she could have attached a separate note with that ghastly letter, explaining her motives. Perhaps even sending her love. But he kissed the top of Valentina's head, and said, "How dear of you to think of that. Thank you. Now, we have something of importance to discuss, and—" He paused and looked up sharply.

The rumble of wheels formed the background for a confused uproar that they would have heard before had they not been so deeply engrossed in each other. "Oh—*no!*" groaned de Michel. "Over a year of waiting, and even now, I cannot have you to myself for longer than a minute or two!"

Following his stricken gaze, Valentina gave a gurgle of laughter. "Your just deserts," she said, standing and offering his cane.

Muttering against the perversity of Fate, de Michel got to his feet while squeals and shouts of excitement rang from the donkey cart.

With his old cob between the shafts, Horace was driving under very crowded conditions. "Sorry sir," he called, grinning broadly. "But they come to the Towers when they heard you was home, and there wasn't no holding 'em. I thought 'twould be best if I was to drive 'em.''

His passengers had already erupted from the cart and with howls and shrieks of glee were galloping towards their target.

"You comed back, Mister Charles! You comed back!"

"We thought as you was dead!"

"Jolly glad you're home, Mister Charles!"

"I baked you a biscuit, Mister Charles, wiv lots o' currants. An' I growed my tooth back—see? Isn't it a lovely one?"

"Tell us all about the war, sir."

"Can we have a game today?"

"Help!" cried de Michel, retreating in apparent horror as they closed in on him.

It was in vain. He was surrounded by leaping, hooting, exuberant children. Eager young arms hugged any part of him they could reach. Joyful voices conveyed with ear-shattering sincerity how much he had been missed. Staggering before that rush of affection, he went down, and was for an instant lost to view. Trying in vain to make herself heard above the shrieks of mirth, Valentina started forward, her amusement banished by anxiety.

His hair and clothing dishevelled, his dark eyes alight with laughter, de Michel reappeared among the tide of beaming faces. "Unhand me—you repellant rascals!" he cried.

This familiar appellation inspired a roar of joy, but the small Jennie pointed out solemnly that Mr. Charles *had* been wounded and they'd "better be

careful with him." Awed, they fell back. He sprawled
there looking up with pseudo-indignation at their re-
pentant faces. "I should think so! A little respect for
the conquering hero, if you please!" Uncertainly, the
grins came back. He grumbled, "Well, don't just look
at me, you silly blocks. Help me up." Their help was
immediate and so unrestrained that Valentina held her
breath. De Michel winked at her as he was restored to
sit against the tree, and his young friends variously
knelt, sat, or jumped around him, bombarding him
with questions.

With a sigh of relief Valentina drew back, a lump
coming into her throat as she watched the heartfelt
welcome, the love so freely exchanged.

Horace tethered the cob and came to join her. "I
hope you didn't mind me bringing 'em here, Miss
Tina. Fair beside themselves they were."

"Of course I didn't mind," managed Valentina,
blinking rather rapidly.

Shouts of mirth resounded and Horace chuckled.
"A fine gentleman, the Lieutenant," he said.

"A very fine gentleman," she agreed proudly, and
knew she was blushing because of the proprietary approval in this faithful man's smile. She called a halt to
the visit then, and banished the childrens' disappoint-
ment by extending an invitation to come to tea at
Wyenott Towers the next afternoon. "Lord Stane will
play rounders with you," she added, as an extra in-
ducement.

"Poor Sam!" exclaimed de Michel laughingly.
"Sold into slavery!"

The children were delighted however, and clambered happily into the cart, calling farewells and thanks as Horace drove them away.

Turning to de Michel, Valentina found him leaning back against the tree, eyes closed, looking thoroughly exhausted. Alarmed, she sank to her knees beside him. "Oh, my dear! Did they—" She was seized in a grip of iron and crushed against him.

"Tactical error," he pointed out with a twinkle.

"Charles! Suppose Horace should turn around!"

"There you go again. I thought I'd cured you of your suppositioning." He tilted up her chin. "Now—do not dare to move, Miss Ashford..."

After a few minutes, she did move, to lie back in his arms and smile up at him dreamily. "You said we had something of importance to discuss," she reminded.

He was concentrating on winding one gleaming ringlet around his finger, and murmured with a shrug, "Oh, it's nothing very important. It can wait."

"Now," she pointed out, "is as good a time as any, Charles."

"I've heard that said before, but it doesn't always apply, you know. However, I shall bow to your superior wisdom. If I can call the matter back to mind." He looked commendably puzzled. "Whatever can it have been, I wonder?"

She tried to sound menacing. "You know perfectly well, sir!"

"Do I? But of course. You're quite correct, my Beautiful Umpire. It was doubtless something about the..."

"The—what, you exasperating creature?"

"The—er, quarry, of course," he said, his eyes guileless. "I'll own I am disappointed in your progress. I'd fancied you would have had it completed by now."

"Had you indeed! Perhaps there is some special reason for haste?"

"Yes, as a matter of fact. I have invited some friends down, since there is to be a ceremony here next week."

"Next *month*, Charles."

"You refer to the marriage of your sister and Sam, which is not the occasion to which I refer. Now what is there in that to make you blush, ma'am? My colonel has agreed to attend this—er, ceremony. And has expressed keen interest in my plans for the quarry. But only look at it! A few wispy trees planted, and some scrawny lawns at the bottom, is all! A forlorn effort, at best!"

"Ungrateful wretch," she scolded, reaching up to tidy a tumbled lock of his dark hair.

He seized her hand and kissed it. "I expect I must give you another extension of time. You always were a slow worker, Miss Ashford."

"Perhaps," she suggested demurely, "were I to change my name, I might do better."

"What—has someone offered, then?"

"Charles...de...Michel!"

Despite a quivering lip, he tried to look mournful. "I suppose, only because I have kissed you on occasion—"

"Several occasions!"

"—I am to be hounded into making an honest woman of you."

"That is very probable, sir."

"Hum." He smiled tenderly into her loving eyes. "Then it is as well I planned the ceremony. Beloved, will you take this silly fellow of tattered repute, small fortune and temperamental disposition, to husband?"

"No," she said. "I will instead, very proudly, accept the offer of the most gallant gentleman I have ever—"

FitzMoke looked around, as if surprised that a lady should have been so rudely interrupted. After a while, he grew tired of waiting for them to continue on to the house. He moved closer and sniffed the brown head and the black which were so very close together, but they chose to ignore his message. Of course, one did not have to wait forever. He would probably be given his carrot even if he went back without them. He ambled hopefully in the direction of the old house.

The little wind grew more chill, and the clouds became ever more grey and threatening, which was odd, because Charles de Michel and his lady forever afterwards remembered that afternoon as one of brilliant sunshine; the most radiant time of their lives.

Harlequin Regency Romance ™

COMING NEXT MONTH

#29 A MERRY GO-AROUND by Coral Hoyle
Kate McClintock was an imposter. In order to save
her father from debtor's prison, she agreed to pose as
the celebrated courtesan the Contessa D'Allesandria
of the Kingdom of Sardinia. Rusticating in
Berefordshire, Kate was certain she would not be in
danger of discovery until Sir Maxim arrived on the
scene. Not only had he been an intimate of the real
courtesan's, but it seemed he was determined to
become intimate with her!

**#30 THE CELEBRATED MISS NEVILLE
by Barbara Neil**
Calvina Nutter had become an overnight success and
was now the toast of the ton. Her second book of
poetry had just been published and everyone eagerly
awaited the critics' response. Sir Rowan Heath,
famous for his scathing political essays, found himself
obliged to issue a cutting review. That was before he
met and fell in love with Catherine Neville and she
very much with him. He had had no way of knowing
Calvina Nutter and Catherine Neville were one and
the same and no hope of ever winning back the only
woman he had ever truly loved.

Harlequin Superromance®

Hamilton
H·O·U·S·E

A powerful restaurant conglomerate that draws the best and brightest to its executive ranks. Now almost eighty years old, Vanessa Hamilton, the founder of Hamilton House, must choose a successor.
Who will it be?

Matt Logan: He's always been the company man, the quintessential team player. But tragedy in his daughter's life and a passionate love affair made him make some hard choices....

Paula Steele: Thoroughly accomplished, with a sharp mind, perfect breeding and looks to die for, Paula thrives on challenges and wants to have it all ...
but is this right for her?

Grady O'Connor: Working for Hamilton House was his salvation after Vietnam. The war had messed him up but good and had killed his storybook marriage. He's been given a second chance—only he doesn't know what the hell he's supposed to do with it....

Harlequin Superromance invites you to enjoy Barbara Kaye's dramatic and emotionally resonant miniseries about mature men and women making life-changing decisions. Don't miss:

• CHOICE OF A LIFETIME—a July 1990 release.
• CHALLENGE OF A LIFETIME
—a December 1990 release.
• CHANCE OF A LIFETIME—an April 1991 release.

Take 4 bestselling love stories FREE

Plus get a FREE surprise gift!

Harlequin Superromance®

A June title
not to be missed....

Superromance author Judith Duncan has created her
most powerfully emotional novel yet, a book about
love too strong to forget and hate too painful to
remember....

Risen from the ashes of her past like a phoenix,
Sydney Foster knew too well the price of wisdom,
especially that gained in the underbelly of the city.
She'd sworn she'd never go back, but in order to
embrace a future with the man she loved, she had to
return to the streets...and settle an old score.

Once in a long while, you read a book that affects you
so strongly, you're never the same again. Harlequin is
proud to present such a book, STREETS OF FIRE by
Judith Duncan (Superromance #407). Her book merits
Harlequin's AWARD OF EXCELLENCE for June 1990,
conferred each month to one specially selected title.

S407-1